GOTHIC TALES & POEMS

By Nathan Reese Maher

1st Edition, June 2019

Copyright © 2019, Nathan Reese Maher

Cover Art by: Nathan Reese Maher
Editor: Harley Maher

GOTHIC TALES & POEMS, All Rights Reserved

No part of this book may be used or reproduced in any manner without explicit written permission, except in the case of brief quotations in critical articles or reviews, from the author.

Printed in the United States.

ISBN – 9781075096044

All characters, places and monsters are a work of fiction and any resemblance to real life is purely coincidental. This book is intended for entertainment and reading pleasure, none of it is real.

TABLE OF CONTENTS

SHORT STORIES

The Sullen Winds Come Calling, pgs. 5-22
Mother, pgs. 23-42
Le Château de Crane, pgs. 43-70
Tales of Enoch – The Watchers, pgs. 71-146

POEMS

Cycle of Mourners, pg. 150
Dance the Macabre, pg. 151
Envy, pg. 152
Gothic Love Poem, pg. 153
Life's Nurturing Embrace, pg. 154
Ode to be my Darkling Child, pg. 155
Oh Savage Night, pg. 156
Remember the Night When the Birds Above, pg. 157
The Gear, Clock and Core, pg. 158
The House with the Painted Door, pg. 159
The Love Once Lost, pg. 160
The Spider of Six, pg. 161
To Jealousy, I Engaged, pgs. 162-163
Twisted Rhyming, Or You Are, pg. 164
Untitled, pg. 165
Untitled 7, pg. 166

SHORT STORIES

The Sullen Winds Come Calling

The night hangs about the exultant landscape accompanied by the harmonious howling of the wind. The thunderheads clap in the distance and light up the cracked window. The porous sill becomes victim to the rain as the water creeps into the bedchamber, collecting into a ghastly puddle upon the floor. The droplets release their sardonic sonance, causing a body to rise hastily from his respite. The cadaver's eyes dart about the room. He watches, shivering from the nightly cold, as his demonic nightmares slip through the cracked windowpane; still clinging to some ghastly remembrance or dream. He surveys what he believes to be his home. The door appears latched and secure, while the furnishings remain exactly as they have before. He pulls his legs up close against his chest and silently listens to the howling of the outside winds. It begins as another sleepless night...

From beneath the beads of sweat that roll down his brow, this older gentleman, a Mr. Henry Cross, glances down toward a space no longer occupied by his dearly beloved. Our venerated hero, age sixty-eight, rocks to the beat of his heart as he watches the rain drizzle into the room. He envisions a time quite similar to the current night, where the howling kept him from his sleep - this jubilant, or more so loathsome, malady of the wind...

Allow me to leave our revered exemplar to his musings as I relay to you the foreground to this venture - Mr. Cross' home is located at the top of a long series of interlocking hills that spring through a forested woodland. His home is a lovely two-story habitation that he had bought for a rather... penniless exchange, with the prospect of rearing a family in the quiet solitude that only an isolated forestry could provide. The original owners had long ago boarded up their adobe; seemingly taken to the allure of the city and had moved without a forwarding address or word of leave. The nearest neighbors (if one would so desire their company) lived nearly fifteen miles away, and without a horse or a suitable form of transportation it would prove one an incredibly journey indeed.

I recall a time when Mr. Cross had decided, after many months of settling in and, by the consigning of his wife, to meet with the contiguous homebodies - to which they replied, as my memory tells me, "We never knew anyone had moved out." But our hero was not much concerned about acquiring the company of others, as the pandemonium of the city did not appeal to him nor did the simple country folk tickle his fancy. His family proved to be more than enough to satisfy his need for companionship and he was, after all, better suited to the ills of isolation.

Here we return to the main character of this tale, which just after he regained his composure from a blissful bed waking, he enters the adjoining bathroom in search of a means to gain a stronger grip on his conscious reality.

He fumbles groggily above the porcelain sink and bares his haunting pallor in the mirror – a ravishing beaut to be sure. His hair had long since fallen to the promise that entropy provided and is scarred in the most ghostly of whites. His skin is laden in the most omnipotent of grooves that only a well-educated age could provide. Yes, our dearest Mr. Cross can be noted for his uncanny charm and excruciating visage – how particularly angelic if anyone could so be named. He raises the sink's handles and splatters an undesirable amount of water into his face. He breathes into a deepened sigh as a parcel of his dream repeats itself in his mind: a thought of running, the glorious scent of alpine breezes assaulting his nostrils, and his distant clamoring as he trips through the forest floor, alerting his pursuer to his flight.

Our faithful Henry shuffles from the upstairs chambers and descends upon a wooden staircase, apparently not minding the impenetrable darkness that resides below. His hands grip tenaciously upon the banister in hopes that the railing will put an end to his fearless trembling – a shaking that persists after such wondrous rouses and is surely a product of such a valiant age. Mr. Cross reaches the parlor of his striking home and makes his way towards the kitchen, a pathway he has been rehearsing since many nights before. Sadly - our illustrious hero wanders to the scattered kerosene lamps, and pilfers a match from a hidden drawer, dousing the marvelous darkness within. He lights the wick from beneath the glass chimney and stabilizes the impending darkness to a dimly lit flame. As his eyes adjust to the crimson glow, he produces a kettle from a lower cupboard, ignites the gas stove and begins to make himself a pot of tea.

He adds to the mixture an old herbal remedy (belladonna, from the smell of it) in hopes of starving out the night with a drug induced slumber, be it hellish or not – so are the bane of sleeping alone. As he waits for the water to boil, our esteemed Mr. Cross glares blankly towards a wall of boards, where solemnly rests a window that makes view of his backyard, a place where he has spent many hours staring; an enticing remembrance of that night long ago. The night was most similar to the one we currently leave our enchanted Mr. Cross, a feral cast of rain and the unrelenting howling gifted by the winds…

Our prized champion rested within the safety of his bed, tucked deliciously within the confines of his pallid sheets. This night he had also woken to an empty bed, but he did not rise nor shift uncomfortably within, as future nights would afford. In fact, the only manner in which he recognized the sudden loneliness of his position was the discomforting warmth that had dissipated from his bedmate, leaving him a disheartening chill. It did not seem unusual to our host (at the time) that his beautiful wife had managed to vanish stealthily into the night without sound or spoken grievance. It was a nightly custom for our Mrs. Cross (Anne was her name, if I recall correctly) to wake suddenly in the midst of the night and make herself a cup of tea - how unbelievably quaint. Henry had reasoned that Mrs. Cross' peculiar ventures lay cause to a lingering family dispute, that had for the previous years, caused her unrest. His ingenious rationality allowed him a decent peace-of-mind in which he gently allowed slumber to overtake him.

In the morning our protagonist woke to find his morning dew still missing from her bed, and evidence proved that she had not yet returned from her nocturnal discourse, as he would have surely noted her return – our Henry is such a perceptive man after all. Perhaps, he had reasoned, that after having her tea and slipping into the comfortable armchair that lay nestled close to the hearth, that she had slipped into a premature repose and he need only but wake her. As he slowly got ready for the day, our beloved Henry devised all sorts of taunts to tease her with, upon her gentle rousing. But as he made his way down the flight of stairs and into the fated parlor, he found not a single breath but his own. The room lay barren, as it were, and only a half-emptied cup gave way to her previous occupation and only the wall clock gave answer to any personal queries. Perhaps, our enlightened fellow thought, that she had woken earlier and decided to have a morning walk to clear the drudgery of the previous night from her head. He thought it queer of her to set off without his knowledge, but led his earlier rationality towards cooking breakfast and setting a place for her at the table in hopes of surprising his belle upon her return.

However, when the hours passed and her food grew cold, with the lingering thoughts of last night's storm, Mr. Cross decided to put on his coat and go look for her. It was not long after he placed his foot over the threshold that his horror began. His heart sank within the prison of his gullet and it raced to a blackened melody. For before his very eyes, lain strewn a few feet from his location were the very fibers of Anne's nightgown, along with a streak of red and disrupted earth that snaked its way farther into the dismal woods.

He clamored from his house, racing into the depths of the fog riddled nightmare, screaming out the name of his dearest beloved. He followed the ghastly trail of crimson wine and torn pieces of flesh – the very ones that would accompany his mind for many days to come. Pressing back the eschewed branches and neighboring thickets, along with an overwhelming sense of nausea that gripped at his throat, Henry finally found his missing bedmate glistening with the reflections of the sunlight off the dark liquids that hung stagnantly about her maimed husk. You would not believe the outpour of terror that betook our hero as he added his stomach's fill to the forests floor, and howled with such intensity that the neighbors would later claim to have heard with detailed accuracy.

The coroner professed that she had been dragged from her home by a pack of lupine beasts, though utterly irregular for this time of year. A hunting party was formed, regardless of the lack of visible tracks, and would after a three-day search, return with not a single pelt or hide. Henry was apologized to for the loss and the people lavished upon him their prayers for times more jubilant (as such days were so easy to come by) and the strength to persevere.

We return to our disturbed patron, Mr. Cross, who is brought back to his conscious reality by being startled from the shriek of the kettle; a warning that it's about to boil over. He finishes the preparation of his tea and takes it to the parlor and finds the solace of his armchair a gratifying treat. After taking a few sips from the porcelain rim, our malevolent hero gets up, opens the chimney chute and stokes a fire within the hearth. He nestles back within the seat of the chair, already feeling the grogginess of the liquid nightshade, and slips into a half-faint while listening intently to the ticks of the wall clock.

He thinks of his son, raising David in the isolation of the hills and forested woodlands, away from the confusion of the city, and away from the influence of nefarious population. He recalls watching him grow, teaching him the many virtues of life that all little boys need to learn. Soon enough, like many blusterous nights before, he begins to watch the apparitions of his memories dance across the parlor – a trick of the lighting no less – and listens as his mind fills the phantoms with a glorious script:

"David, the city is a horrid place filled with terrible things that try and tempt a man's soul. Here in the woods we are safe from the temptations of vice, safe from the jaws that wait to consume those who partake in its luxuries."

His phantom son, a boy of six years in age, looks upon his father like a grand protector and a saint, "The city sounds scary father. I want to stay here with you and mommy forever."

He then hears the howling of the wind as it rattles against his shutters and remembers another night…

This night was filled with the same sullen weather as the current, a time where he and wife sat in the very room that Mr. Cross now inhabits. A time when his son grew discontent with the lonesome travail of his existence and wished to brave the city for a night or so, but his father would hear nothing of it:

"Why won't you let me go to the city and see it for myself?" Our now sixteen-year-old David proclaimed rebelliously.

"The city is not a place for a boy like you! You are still young and do not know the way of the world. I forbid you from leaving this house!"

"Of course I don't, you keep me in here without letting me go out and discover it for myself! I hate being cooped up in here!"

"When you are older you will understand what I am telling you and you will thank me for it."

Our hero was called a fool by his discourteous son, a man shadowed by the passing of time, unable to stare into the eye of the beast that swells in the heart of a city. But as it is known, our champion is dauntless in his age and did not allow the insult to his pride carry for long. The boy was cast out into the night, to spend the night with the "beast" he so longed for (those beautiful nocturnal creatures no doubt) and only when he would learn his lesson would he be welcomed back. Besides, Henry believed that if his son proved resilient against the hungry storm than perhaps it would quench his desires for adventure. He would come back a changed boy, grateful for his father's hospitality, aged wisdom and company. The only thing was is that he did not come back. The boy did not return as was originally anticipated and days turned to years and not a single word was heard— Oh how the guilt ravaged our poor and beloved hero, for truly he had none other to blame but himself, and he carried it through the ages like a cracked shield.

Now he carries two losses upon his heart: a belated wife and a missing son. He was sure that, upon hearing of his mother's death, that the boy would return to him and he would finally be given a second chance to apologize for the deed he had wrought, but to no avail. The years continued to pass unheeded by forgiveness and our sweet dearest Mr. Cross drew more and more inside himself, till that one day when he finally had enough of this world; he boarded up his windows and locked himself within his home, a prisoner to his own nightmares.

Mr. Cross' eyes began to flutter and with half the tea already absorbed within his system, the ticks of the clock lulled our drugged host to slumber…

He dreamed of a horde of ravishing wolves descending

upon him, lashing out with their claws and rending him fully with daggers from their maw. The sound of his precious ichors splatter against the forest floor, much like the sound that issued upon his intestinal upheaval on the day he had found his wife. He screams as his tendons rip from his muscles and are swallowed into the gullets of the sadistic beasts, the inevitable feeling of dread encompasses his body, as he is no longer able to fight off the frenzy. All he is able to hear is the sound of his heart knocking at his chest, feeling as if though it were going to burst from his ribs and out into the mouth of the nearest beast. Anxiety pours from the pounding of his heart. It gets louder the more blood he loses, the more blood, the faster they consume his flesh, and the faster they consume, the louder his heart pounds; louder and then louder, the door—

He awakes in a tainted dream-like state where even the furnishings appear vaporous. His drug-induced quiescence still cling to his perceptions and it would be a few moments before he could regain his full recognition. The night still flurries about him like a cyclone, the winds ram themselves against the foundation, his home still groaning against the intensities of their punishments. The fire within his hearth had dimmed to mere embers which occasionally flicker with life. Mr. Cross did not realize, or perhaps did not make the immediate connection between the pounding in his dream and that upon his door. Alas, in lieu of the room's shifting nature, our swaying host makes quick to reanimate the cinders and throws on a few logs for good measure. He clenches at his temples, massaging the throbbing points, in an ill attempt at exorcising the dream from his mind.

Our prudent Mr. Henry Cross is startled by a pounding by which causes his heart to once again catch within his throat. He drops the iron poker that he had been previously using to stoke the dying flames and clenches the back of the chair, gripping at the quiver in his heart – as he is in such a vulnerable age. He glares fully at the barred door, thrice locked by several latches that he had installed not a few months before. He looks, then toward the plywood windows, ensuring that every board is in place – none so moved an inch. The old man bites his teeth together and stares without motion, dreading the very noise that he heard within his dream now incarnate behind his front door. He waits and listens to the winds' lament as they crash against the dreary boards that block entrance from his windows hoping… just wishing that whatever decorous villain awaits his answer would see no sense too it, and eventually conclude that no one was home and inevitably seek sanctuary elsewhere. However, the knocking does not cease, but only becomes more violent as the winds picks up and the rain continues to pour.

Henry creeps with an almost cat-like grace – an astounding feat for such an age, if I would ever be so bold – and delivers a slight whisper beneath the crack of the door, "Who's there…?"

Obviously from the majestic howling that encompasses the exterior world, that there would be no way possible, except for those of the most keenest of hearing, to be able to understand the susurrate of our gifted orator Mr. Cross and therefore no spoken reply is issued, save for another volley of rigorous knocking at the base of his door.

Taken aback by the frightening jostle, our host scuttles backwards, stops in a crab-like position and challenges the fiend once more, "Who's there!" And this time louder than before – and much more confidant, I might add. Nevertheless, the door remains silent, not a single voice or recognizable sound is uttered save that of the persistent groaning storm. Our hero is dumbfounded and simply shakes from his malleable contortion, and repeats his demand after another full two-rotations of ticks that issue from the wall clock, "WHO IS THERE!?"

The night continues to stir warily about the house and he can hear the foundation creaking under the stress of

Mother Nature. He relaxes his muscles as he pushes himself against a far wall that is erected directly across the grievous door, and he stares at the hard oaken gateway in an anxious anticipation that made cause for him to rock back and forth at the wall clock's dictations – a true man of melody. It is not before long (perhaps an hour or so) that the still lingering effect of his previously ingested "remedy" begins to toil upon his eyelids, and after a strenuous pause of nothing, our man simply drifts off into sleep.

He dreams about a couple of nights after his son had not returned, a night for when his afflicted Anne gave into a mother's sorrow…
"Where is David? What happened to my poor dear boy?! If something has happened to him I swear to you Henry, that I'll never forgive you! What were you thinking - throwing him out into the night with no place to go? What kind of father are you? What kind of man would deny his own son a warm bed to sleep in? You're nothing but a monster!"
Our venerated hero wakes to the sound of a light tapping against a hidden pane, and with the winds having died to a modest volume, captivates his intrigue. He gets up from his uncomfortable post and realizes that the planks that cover the hidden glass have been removed, leaving him vulnerable to the nefarious tapping. Perhaps a tree limb or a little bird seeking shelter for the night, he thought to himself as he crawls cautiously towards the hypnotic rapping. Drawing himself up upon the windowsill, he gazes out into the night, squinting to make better light in piercing the darkness that the forest is providing. Unable to make note of anything out of the usual, our perceptive detective presses his face against the windowpane, in hopes of extending his view. A snarling silhouette dips its nose against the glass from the opposite side, its eyes glowing with a horrific red, fogs the clear glass with the insatiable heat of its breath. Henry backs from the fiendish head, just as the human-like demon keens at

him, flashing its gnarled teeth.

The creature removes itself from the window, and crashes headlong through the glass and into our petrified Mr. Cross, gnashing and clawing viciously at his huddled form as the glass scatters about them. Mr. Cross's shirt is seized in the consternation, the being's hands decayed and deformed, pulls him from his home, through the window, and into the darkness. He is assaulted by the smell of fresh soil and the grave…

Mr. Cross awakens once more, but this time the windows' barriers still cling securely to the wall. The wind had in deed died down, and only a whimsical breeze whistled into the night air. The fire had smoldered once again to fine ash and embers and our dearest Henry is left with nothing but the light seeping from the kitchen to find his way. As he stands, he rubs the muscles that he knows will later prove to handicap him and he turns towards the staircase that leads to his upstairs bedroom. As he reaches the first step, his nerves are assaulted by an intensive pounding issuing yet again outside his door. He turns awestruck with terror, unbeknownst until now that the previous knocking at the door was not another of his erratic nightmares and in fact still lingered at his threshold.

It was not until the second set of knocks that betook our hero to answering once again, "Have you no decency to rouse an old man at this late hour! I warn you – I am armed!" Our devoted Mr. Cross had never fired a gun (nor owned one for that matter) in his entire life.

The wind stirred with an auspicious nature and it was but an extremely short pause until the being would answer, "Hello? Is there someone there?" It was a masculine voice (pleasant enough I'd imagine) that held a musical ring to it (possibly a baritone). And though even laced with flowered pleasantries, our insatiably rude Mr. Cross refuses to allow or even bid the nice stranger entry into his home - instead he feels it quite in his right to lend himself to xenophobia.

"I'm sorry I'm not allowing any visitors, please go away!"

The wind groans in slight agitation before the stranger is able to speak again, "I'm sorry to bother you but I am looking to see if a Mr. Henry Cross lives here. I was told that this place was condemned but I have a couple people here with me that claim that they know you."

"I've told you already! I'm not permitting any visitors!" Our delectable morsel replies. "I don't care who you have with you. Please go away."

The winds quiet to an unsettling calmness and our host now inches his way closer to the door. His feet gently drift across the parlor as if he himself an apparition – he amazes me even now as to the silence of his footfalls.

"But sir, we have traveled a long way. Could you not permit us–"

Henry slams his fist against the wooden monolith of a door and screams, "GO AWAY!"

I am not sure as to whether or not our faithful hero was having a bad reaction to the belladonna, or perhaps his dreams were placing him a bit too far on edge, or maybe it all boiled down to simple frustrations - Mr. Cross, after all, was not known for his social aptitude.

The wind, seemingly impatient in its circulations, begins a low-pitched whine that strikes our hero with such a chill that he automatically attributes it towards the supernatural and pulls himself violently from the door. He waits, staring intensely at the fibers of the portal, with the oddest inclination that if he were to stare in just the right manner that he could see past the oak barrier and perceive the stranger on the opposite side. However, it is known that beings such as Mr. Cross are incapable of the feat, and thus his mind, still unable to see past the wooden structure, begins to weave all sorts of terrors.

The silence that continues allows him to concoct a

variety of evils that he believes, at this very moment, stalks the outside of his home, searching for some manner of entry, a place that he had somehow forgotten to barricade. A full ten minutes go by, and a vicious howling erupts from the ghostly silence of the night, the wind begins to pick up once again and a plea erupts from beyond the front door, "Mr. Cross, I beg of you. We've been outside in the storm. We're cold, wet, and tired, and if it would not be too much to ask, to allow us inside for just tonight. I'm fearful that we are within the eye of the storm and it shouldn't be much longer for it to return."

Our illustrious champion, our lord amongst lords, contemplates the sincerity of the noble stranger and though guilt-stricken as Mr. Cross is, still utterly refuses to offer the travelers sanctuary. "No! I'm sorry. I can't let you in. I want to let you in, but I simply can't. Please go away and trouble me no more."

The wind circles the house with a vindictive moan and the foundation responds with a similar response. The shutters creak as the wind grows more intense while the moments press on. Our hero crumbles to his knees and sits most valiantly in his pose. If he had been a religious fellow, he would have cupped his hands in prayer for those who were trapped on the opposite side, but alas he was not; not religious in the least. So our dearest and beloved Henry sits within his righteous stance and a tear drops from his eye.

"Mr. Cross, I have someone here who wishes to speak with you. Perhaps he can persuade you better than I can..." There is a pause. The wall clock ticks a few measures before a second voice is heard, this one a bit higher – a tenor perhaps...

"Dad?"

Henry's face, what was once turned down in pity, now slowly raises his head to confront the skip in his heartbeat.

"Dad is that you? It's me, David."

Henry echoes his son's name in but a whisper, mouthing the name as if speaking some forbidden language.

"It's been a long time since I've seen you dad. I know

when we last parted it wasn't on the best of terms."

"You were supposed to come back!" Henry slams his hand bitterly against the hardwood floor. "You left your mother and me all alone up here. Do you know what that did to us?"

The wind squalls into the night air, the ferocity shakes the foundation, the windows' shutters slam against the siding and the embers from his hearth sweep outwards and onto the bare floor. Henry cringes from the sudden jolt of air and scrambles backwards against the wall.

"Look, this probably isn't the best way to talk about this. If you would let me in, I promise you that I will explain everything, my decision, where I went, what I've done with my life… everything. Okay? Now would you please open the door and let us in? It's getting cold out here. I don't know how much longer we can stand it."

Our host's lip quivers as he speaks, internally he fights with the desire of opening the door and rushing to embrace his long lost son, but the fear of storm – Yes! The fear of the wind, the utter howling of the wind and the beasts that dwell outside drives our cowardly hero into staying his hand and condemning his son to a dreadful fate that the night would inevitably grant.

"I'm sorry!" He shouts with a torrent of tears, "I can't let you inside. You don't understand! You just don't understand!" The night once again fills with a wailing, but this time emitting from a poor wretch of a creature – our fallen Mr. Henry Cross has finally teetered off the edge. He finds himself to be a pathetic being, sitting there across the door from his very salvation and incapable of unlatching the very locks he himself had installed; far too drawn away from the realities of the world – who could possibly blame him?

The wind wails a treacherous sound that causes the parlor to cry out in a fit of agony. A distant thunderhead rolls across the forested woodlands, the peacefulness of the eye slowly dwindles as our dishonorable paladin strives to reclaim his composure. He dries his tears on the sleeve of his night robe and gazes longing at the gateway before him.

"Dad, I have someone else here who would like to talk to you, okay?" A short pause persisted once again, an unbearable silence that left our protagonists heart on the verge of halting all together.

Then he heard her voice and his entire body went numb, his hands clammed up to the point that he could no longer move. A thick lump caught in his throat and he could feel himself suffocating.

"Henry...? Henry is that you?"

He dreamed of hearing that voice for many years, he remembered every intonation; the rise and fall of her sweet soprano voice. It was the voice of his dearly belated.

"Anne?"

"Yes, Henry it's me. Can you please let me in? It's incredibly cold out here and storm has made me tired."

"No! It can't be you!" His voice trembles. "You're dead! This isn't real! This isn't real!"

Her voice fills with concern, "I didn't die! What on earth are you talking about?"

"The wolves, I saw it with my own eyes. You were torn to pieces by the wolves!" The memory slowly begins to shape within his mind.

"The wolves? Henry, listen to me. There are no wolves. I didn't die. I left you, Henry. I had to go find our son. Please let me in so that I can prove this to you."

Henry's heart races at such a speed that one would suspect that without the aid of the nightshade, his heart surely would have imploded on itself. He shakes his head in disbelief, remembering the horrid visage that burned into his mind on the day he had found her body, the very image that would haunt him in his dreams for the rest of his nocturnal life.

"No! No! This can't be real. This can't be real! I saw you dead! I saw what they did to you. I saw the blood! I followed it into the forest. I found you laying there... I found your remains—oh, God!" He nearly avoids vomiting as he recalls the scene in his mind, the acrid taste of his own stomach clenches to the back of his throat.

"Henry, I didn't die. Please, why won't you believe me?" She begins to sob, "Please Henry open the door, don't make yourself suffer any longer alone. I've come back for you sweetheart, we both have. Please just open the door and be reunited with your family. Everything will be alright. I promise it will. Just open the door. I'm sorry I had to run out on you. I couldn't take not seeing David, I had to find out on my own if he was okay. But I found him, and now everything is going to be like it once was, we can be together again. A family."

Tears stream down his cheeks like the sanguine liquid that had poured from his wife's mangled cadaver. He slowly begins to inch his way, as a palatable crab with his hands behind his back, scurrying his way closer to the foot of the door.

The wind howls, dashing its fullest violence against the house, causing the door to rattle within its hinges. He hears a scream from beyond his threshold, a noise that sends him flying to the rescue. Anne's wailing dissipates amidst that of the winds as the door pounds against its fragile hinges, matching the rhythm of his palpitating heart.

"Hold on Anne!" He shouts as he unlatches the first last. "I'm coming David!" The second is withdrawn shortly after.

An unearthly calm descends upon the night as our redeemed hero withdrawals the final latch of his oaken door. His hand trembles from the delirium of the deed, unaware of the disheartening silence that swells about the parlor, the wall clock fastens to the moment, as he reaches for the handle. With a hard swallow, the pounding still reverberating within his head, our exquisite champion inhales a deep courageous breath and opens the oaken door...

It would be unbecoming of me if I left you in a bewildered sense, in believing that our venerated Mr. Cross had prevailed over some touchstone of his life. However, if you would be so kind as to allow me to relate to you the entirety of the affair, I can promise you an easy respite for future nights to come:

Well you'll see that our beloved Mr. Cross, after opening that fateful door, adopted a face so cleverly mixed with an awe-struck horror – a face that one could never again expect to see in a single lifetime. For what stood before him was not the anticipated forms of his wretched family, but instead a being so god-like, so intermingled with his nightmares, that he gave a ghastly shriek that nearly stole the very lifeblood that the creature had conspired to steal. The beast was abhorrent to behold, a six-foot demonic spirit that took the form of a silver furred loup garou whose fangs dripped of discordant ooze and eyes that raged with such an intense ferocity that all the blood of the countryside could never quench. However, it was not the beast itself that stole his blood-tainted parlor, for pressing in a tormented fashion, stretching outwardly from the creature's skin were hundreds of faces, all fighting to be free from beneath; among them his beloved family.

"You were right dad," the David visage spoke, a mouth filled with flesh, "I learned my lesson. Can I please come home now?"

From the creature's shoulder spoke Anne, "I'm sorry Henry, I shouldn't have been so harsh. Please forgive me."

The rest of the faces were all jeering, all smiling at the angst-ridden soul of Mr. Cross as they pushed his family's faces deeper within the beast until they could no longer be seen, swallowed by a sea of features. With a single lunge, the creature gripped him by his throat and dragged the delicacy down a familiar path that Mr. Cross had stalked many years before. His screams, though legendary at best, were no match for the baying that ensued as he was thrown to banquet. I cannot remember a time when a meal such as this would be savored by the beast – as the suspense, I attest, adds to the flavor.

After the horrendous gore, when the feast of blood soaked into the blackened earth, another tormented face fought its way to the creature's epidermis and howled ghoulishly into the night. It would not be long until the aghast'd visage of Henry Cross was pushed back within the creature's body, consumed by a jumble of expressions and voices that all climbed atop one another selfishly to be seen.

Whenever anyone asks about the poor old man who used to live within the ancient abandoned house, the neighbors simply shrug their shoulders and say, "We never knew anyone had moved out." It is assumed that his beloved family had, without reason or word, returned to enjoy the luxuries of the city. As you see, the city now stands outside Mr. Cross' front door. The paved roads, the lumbering skyscrapers, the dashing of cars, the speeding of trains, and the many many hungry voices of the nefarious population.

So here I now lament this gruesome tale, anticipating the days when the night is fresh, when new blood purchases a home in hopes of escaping the complexities of the city. There they will enjoy the comforts that only an isolated forestry can provide, until that one night when those sullen winds come calling and the city comes knocking at their door.

Mother

In all the world — as wishes tend to be worded — I would like nothing more than to fall into the apron of the one they call, mother. Father rarely spoke of her, and when he did, it took the courage of hard whiskey to get him sober enough to ask. Even then I could only make out a few words from his ramblings, none of which have been helpful to my understandings. My father wasn't well, you see, as he would spend his days locked in his room while he howled painfully through the hours. And during the night, he would try and peek at me from beneath the cracks of my door, making sniffing noises, and whispering my mother's name, "Rochellè... Rochellè..." He'd open my door slightly and just stand there, looking at me for hours, with his head and limp limbs to one side. I'd pretend to be asleep, afraid of what he might do had he known I was awake. He never moved. He never blinked. Near morning he'd call out like a squalled spirit and shamble slowly back to his room. Only then, would I be able to calm my nerves and revel in a few hours of uninterrupted sleep. Like I said, my father wasn't well.

I do not understand how it happened, but one day my father was gone. That same day they came for me. They told me he was sick and would be in the hospital for a while. I wasn't allowed to see him. They packed my things for me and shipped me off to St. Ambrose Orphanage and Sisterhood, where I was told I would be placed into gentler hands.

The Sisters there held themselves highly, and would look down at my thin body while whispering to one another – "Watch that one! She comes from touched breeding." My reputation didn't improve when during my welcoming interview with Mother-Superior Sister Aubrey turned sour after I asked who God was. I think it was the question about my baptism – or lack of the event – that sparked tensions between me and the Sisters of St. Ambrose that day. When the offer came for me to be accepted into the waters, I refused; solely on the basis that since my mother hadn't deemed it necessary, why would I require it now? I think it was the manner of my speech, or that the refusal may have been misconstrued as demeaning, that the revered Mother Aubrey spouted quite matter-of-factly, that since my mother had committed suicide shortly after my birth, that she couldn't have been in the "right state of mind" to determine what was proper for a girl of my age. I cried through the rest of the interview.

My stay in the orphanage would have been far more difficult had it not been for Sister Clara. As far as I understood it, Sister Clara was Mother Aubrey's closest confidant and the next in line should Mother Aubrey be called home. All the other Sisters were weary around her, and chose their words carefully, as if in fear of the retributions they'd suffer if their gossips reached the Mother-Superior's ear. The fact of the matter is, that Sister Clara held a spiritual piety that even a blasphemer, such as myself, could appreciate. She was meek. She was soft. She was acquiescent. She had eyes that could hush the most tormented of souls – a pair I had wished my father could have beheld, as perhaps it would have done him some good. She flashed me the occasional smile, which I'd associate to what my mother's would have looked like. To my misfortune, Sister Clara would always be busy with one chore or another and her visits would be brief, leaving me to the discretions of the other Sisters.

There'd be times when I was allowed to roam free about the orphanage, to learn the layout of the differing classrooms, kitchen, and converted dormitories intended for both Sister and orphan alike. Some of the doors were closed off to me, and when I inquired about them I was told, with rather grim distaste toward my presence, that they had been sealed due to structural integrities until such a time when they'd be renovated – it was an orphanage after all and money came only in charities. During our lessons, the Sisters pledged that modesty was one of the greatest of human virtues and should be practiced on a daily basis. But their rooms were palaces in comparison to the single rooms, each occupied by fourteen children with nothing but a cot to sleep on and a rusty trunk to keep our remembrances in. Their rooms were filled with bookshelves, armoires, baubles, and beds large enough to fit at least four of us comfortably. I made the mistake of pointing this out during an oration – all in the spirits of modesty – and for my insights, I was forced to sit in a corner. One cannot blame the Sisters for their strict-cruelties, as they were trying their best to teach an edict which was purely contradictory to a person's nature.

There were times, no matter how hard I struggled, that I would run off and cry by myself, and if one of the Sister's caught me, I would be dragged by the back of my neck to see Mother-Superior for her to evaluate my sanity and likely punishment. Making friends at St. Ambrose was difficult for me. All the other orphans felt that their existence was rife with troubles enough, without adding me to their list. The majority of the time I preferred to be alone. However, even that would attract the Sisters attention as a sign of instability and so I would be forced to play with the others, despite their displeasure, to ensure the Sisters of my good health.

However, there was one orphan who caught my attention, a girl named Sarah Flancey. She had gorgeous blonde hair, which was naturally wavy, that reached the middle of her back. Her skin was the color of cream and she wore white batiste dresses whenever she could. The other Sisters were careful around her, as much as they were with Sister Clara, as I learned later that Sarah was Sister Aubrey's favorite and would spend many hours giving her private tutorage. In fact, I later discovered, through the gossips of the other Sisters, that the majority of Sarah's wardrobe came from the Mother-Superior herself! I was lucky to live in the same room as Sarah, let alone breathe the same air. I watched her as often as I could without rousing suspect of my interest. I learned many things without her knowing, such that she hummed whenever she was alone or getting dressed; at times she would curtsey to the phantoms in her head, pretending she was in royal court or a part of some prestigious retinue; she also loved to play games of logic, such as Stop-Gate, All the Kings Horses, and Rim. At night, while all the other children were asleep, Sarah would creep from her bed and out into darkness of St. Ambrose. She wouldn't return until early morning, just shy of the crack of dawn. One night, I decided to follow her, and shadowed her all the way to Sister Aubrey's room where she was greeted by the Mother-Superior. I managed to tip-toe my way to the door and peer through the keyhole just long enough to see the two get beneath the covers and turn off the lights. Like before, Sarah returned; where she would slide between the linen of her cot and pretend that she'd been sleeping there all night.

The thought of being welcomed into Sister Clara's bed, much the same way Sarah had been in Sister Aubrey's, was warming to me. I wanted nothing more than to acquire Sister Clara's love and attentions, to be doted upon, and be taken in for private tutorage. Above all else I wanted that thing that all orphans dream, to feel the euphoric embrace of their Mother – regardless of whom it came from.

So I began my secret affair, to entice and furthermore woo the unsuspecting Sister into my favor. I would watch her between lessons to learn her well-kept schedule and offer my help whenever I had the chance. In this she was delighted and would bare one of her generous smiles that would make one think she was giving you a gift. My contributions included sweeping the floors, scrubbing hard to reach places, running from place to place with notes or assignments for the other Sisters – who would receive them with bitterness. They'd tell me, "My, aren't you helpful today" and would then steal a glance from one of the other Sisters as if to communicate some terrible thought. But I didn't care, as I was happy to be in the service of Sister Clara and I would suffer lightly beneath the other Sisters' discretions.

My plan to show Sister Clara my usefulness didn't quite get the results that I had intended, as my reward would be a simple thank you and then her sending me off to fulfill my daily lessons. I anticipated that she wouldn't welcome me directly, and might take a few days to warm up to my presence, but after a week of errands, and still the invitation to share her bed hadn't arisen, I became impatient. I decided to increase my resolve and work even harder to gain her approval, but it seemed that the Sisters' God decided to work against me, as every time I would do something nice it would fail miserably due to some blundering on my part: I would try and carry water for the kitchen but end up spilling it everywhere; I picked a beautiful bouquet of flowers for Sister Clara's hair, and was scolded for vandalizing the garden; I'd even try to wash a few articles of Sister Clara's clothing, but ended up ruining them completely! All my troubles and sacrifices only proved to hinder my relationship with Sister Clara, and no matter how hard I tried to get her to see my love, it only served to push her further and further away. Then the unthinkable! the cruelest lie to have ever escaped the lips of the Sisters of St. Ambrose – a rumor of the most despicable and vilest sort: that my actions were woven to appear as desperate acts from a mentally deranged girl! They made me sound like a demon forged to torment the good graces of Sister Clara, that I was obsessed! such to the point that they fancied her a victim, and when word reached Mother-Superior I was brought before her and told I was to never to speak or further bother Sister Clara again. I returned to my room where I wept there for days without any comfort or call to join the rest of the children –I was officially an outcast.

Then one night, as I struggled for comfort against my tear-soaked pillow, Sarah returned after only a few moments leave from her bed, but this time she walked with a dreary, loose composure, that was reminiscent of my father's own drudgeries. Instead of slipping beneath the covers like so many times in the past, she just sat on her cot and stared with her back to me, looking at nothing in particular for hours. I thought that she was deep in contemplation, or had been scolded for some offense; I didn't pay it any heed. I happened to fall asleep that night, but woke the next morning with Sarah still sitting in the same place, refusing to budge – pale from the chill of the previous night. The other children were afraid of her, and called the Sisters into our room thinking that she may be sick. While the rest of the children were gathered and sent off to their lessons - and while I was told to simply vacate the room - two of the Sisters were watching over her, checking her temperature and debating whether they should call for a doctor.

When my chores were over and the lessons were still in session, I returned to the dormitory to see how she was doing. I found her staring at the ceiling, on her back, and tucked tightly beneath the covers of her cot. They were so tight in fact that it appeared like she was suffocating beneath them. But I was too afraid to loosen them for fear she'd leap at me. She still looked pallid and I wondered what had transpired to cause her such a degradation in health. I gathered my courage and snuck up to her bedside. I was partially unnerved by how her eyes refused to remove themselves from that haunting stare, even as I sat beside her. I whispered silently at first, to clear the knot in my throat that had begun to form, and then loud enough that only her and I could hear, "Sarah – Are you okay?" and when she wouldn't answer, not even a blink for my efforts, I was immediately reminded on how my father would stare, and how at times I would try to wonder exactly what he was thinking. As I was about to leave – too frightened to stay any longer – her throat released a low chilling moan before gasping for air, whispering in an almost pleading fashion, " Who would be my Mother now?" I cried as she cried, tears streaming down the sides of her face, while still staring at the ceiling – never blinking at some horrendous stream of thought that I can only try to imagine. The thought was far too upsetting for me to bear, and I fled from the room with her whispers still echoing inside my head.

I had troubles sleeping the next night, as all I could do is lay awake, while occasionally sending a glance over at Sarah who was still staring at the ceiling. She hadn't made a sound since I had last left her earlier that day. I couldn't help but feel guilty for leaving her, as I am sure I'd been the only person she had spoken to since her illness. Sarah was the girl that I envied, but now I could do nothing more than pity her. Still, I felt like we had some kind of a connection, a bond that was forged the moment we shed tears together. But out of the darkness of our room, came a soft giggling that arose from Sarah's cot; an insatiable laughter that must have bothered the other children, as I could hear the constant sounds of shifting in their beds. Her giggling lasted for an hour, something which drove the other children to lie nervously awake. I feared that if she became any louder she'd wake the entire occupancy of St. Ambrose. And so I snuck from my cot and slowly maneuvered around the other children's beds, all the while they watched me from beneath their pillows with wide-eyed apprehension. She continued to giggle, even after I peeked my head over her bedside and tried to hush her by placing my finger over her lips. Sarah persisted, her eyes still trapped in whatever thought she had conjured up for herself, and I could do nothing but continually strive to snap her out of it. I brushed the hair out of her eyes and felt the softness of her cheeks – she was cold. No longer afraid of her condition, and more concerned for the well-being of the other orphans, I decided to loosen Sarah's covers and cuddle inside with her. She acted as if she didn't notice my intrusion, or if she did it didn't bother her. I tried to comfort her as best as I could, wrapping my arms around her in desperation to keep Sarah warm and to keep her quiet. The cot was cramped, but somehow, I managed to find a comfortable spot. Her giggling waned, dwindling only as the warmth returned to her face. It wouldn't be until roughly another hour before the laughter finally ended, and Sarah was fast asleep.

We continued like this for a couple weeks. At first Sarah was still trapped in her stare, but after awhile I would notice her blink or that she would turn to her side instead of staring at the ceiling constantly. During the moments when she'd start to cry silently to herself, I'd cozy up to her and hold her as best as I was able and she'd eventually stop and be able to sleep peacefully. If the sisters new about the intensive care that I was giving her, they didn't show it, nor give as much as an estranged looked – as I'm sure that they appreciated not having to tend to Sarah as well as being overburdened by all the rest of their daily responsibilities. I was left completely alone and instead of going to my lessons I would sit at her bedside and read to her, drape a cold cloth over her forehead, and make sure that she had everything she needed. It wasn't long until Sarah started to become her old self again, and we'd have conversations together – but it still took quite a while before she was well enough to rejoin the rest of the children. During which time I would challenge her to those games of logic she loved so much, and I would lose every time, but I didn't care. We'd stay up late at night huddled beneath the covers and talked about our philosophy on life, but most of the times indulged ourselves in making fun of the Sisters and their predispositions with one another. By the end of it, once she was well enough to take trips outside of the dormitory and finally be capable of returning to her daily routine, I found that I had finally made a friend – a friend of whom I could share my deepest secrets with. I never left her side.

Things were going well until the nightmares came. Sarah started to have difficulty sleeping, and while I would drift off to sleep next to her, she would lay awake thinking of one thing or another. At times I would wake and found that she had somehow slipped from the confines of our cot and would sit in one of the window sills looking out into the darkness. When she'd realize that I was awake, she would try to sooth me back to sleep, and despite my urgings for her to return, she'd continue to stare out into the darkness – occasionally nodding to some distant voice that I couldn't hear. When Sarah did sleep, she tossed and turned, shaking her head to avoid some nefarious denizen hiding in the realm of dreams. I'd struggle to wake her, and when she opened her eyes they were wide with indescribable terror that she would cling to me, her hands desperately grabbing at my clothing as if her grip were slipping away off some precipice. I comforted her as best as one could, but there was nothing I could do – as she was being assaulted by some manner of inner-conflict that I was incapable of altering. All I could do was sit with her and rock with her back and forth, stroking her hair to get her to stop shaking, enough that she'd be able to fall back asleep.

One night I awoke to find Sarah gone. She wasn't in the room and I feared that she had wandered off somewhere in flight of a horrifying dream. I didn't go out to look for her, as St. Ambrose, despite the close-quarters and living arrangements, was large – filled with plenty of nooks and crannies that one could hide in if they didn't wish to be found. She'd return the next morning, just shy of dawn, like she had so many times in the past. I was afraid she was returning to sleep with the Mother Superior, but after a few nights of her reoccurring disappearing act, I soon learned that Mother Aubrey had vanished! Everyone was affected, the Sisters were a little on edge, the orphans were afraid that something terrible had befallen her – and even the local police were called to uncover her whereabouts. We all were questioned, but no one could place what had happened, or where she might have gone. Though strangely Sarah wasn't affected by it, she'd answer the questions just like anyone else, but would relate that with her recent sickness, that she hadn't been able to fall back in with her usual habits and hadn't the slightest idea of where she could have gone. Mother Superior's disappearance disturbed me for some reason, despite any ill feelings, and even more so that Sarah wasn't. I reasoned that she knew something the rest of us didn't, and thus why she was relatively unconcerned when approached about it. Perhaps the Nun-Mother couldn't take the isolation of St. Ambrose any longer and decided to quit her duties – that was at least the popular theory, but it didn't explain why she hadn't packed any of her things. When the police questioned me, I decided to leave out the parts about Sarah's nightly rendezvous with Sister Aubrey – don't ask me why. After a few days of continuous questions by both the police and Sisters, the newspapers chalked it up as a "Runaway Nun" and lessons proceeded as normal. I was pleased to hear that Sister Clara became the new Mother Superior for I knew, as my history tends to repeat, that I'd be sent into her folds once my sanity was thought to have slipped. To my surprise, the rest of the cloister became lax in their strict duties and I was able to slip kindly by without attracting the evil eye.

    A few days later, as Sarah and I were enjoying a break from our lessons, she told me of a wonderful game she had just invented called Mother Knows Best. The game was similar in concept to Simon Says, except that the length of time spanned throughout the day and sometimes even the night. Sarah would tell me a list of things that needed to be done, like tiny chores outside of what the Sisters gave us, and she'd have an equal number of chores as well. Who would ever get the majority of these tasks completed by the next day would become Mother's favorite. Accordingly, if I became Mother's favorite, Sarah would let me in on a little secret she's been keeping and allow me to designate the tasks the next day. For weeks we'd play, the both of us given a set number of tasks to complete, fairly equal in proportion, but somehow Sarah would always be the one to have finished the most. After suspecting she had been cheating, I followed her without her knowing and learned that she had been enlisting the other children to perform the tasks for her! When I approached her about it, she was quick to point out that as long as the tasks were done and done properly, that she still qualified to be Mother's favorite. Sarah was keeping a running tally and took every opportunity to rub it in my face on how she was the favored one. Not only was I determined to beat her at her own game, but I was very curious as to what secret she was keeping from me – as it was her way of further enticing me to play. She was manipulative, I give her that. So I had to become even more manipulative in order to get the children to accomplish my tasks instead of hers.

Each night Sarah would sneak off, and when I asked her where she was going, she told me it was to form the new list. I asked if I could come with her, but her face turned frightful and she screamed "No!" in such a way that it terrified me. Amazingly yet, her countenance shifted to the serene and said that it would ruin the secret she had in store for me and besides, I needed all the sleep I could get to win tomorrow's game. I didn't want to anger her further and so, with reluctance, I fell back asleep. One day I came close to Sarah's total, but she grew bored and decided to change the rules. The tasks turned mischievous in nature, such as stealing the lesson plan from an orating Sister, or pilfering snacks from the kitchen. Instead of whoever finished the majority of the tasks, it was whatever prank was deemed to carry the most weight. And since I wasn't comfortable with letting the two of us be the judges, I insisted that since we'd acquired a small following of admirers (as manipulations tend to accrue) that they'd better serve as mediators. Sarah was tickled but bargained that they still had a part in the pranks as to ensure discretion and prevent tattle-tailing.

And so our game continued! While I secretly added too much starch to the Sisters wardrobe, Sarah would counter it by greasing the inside doorknob to every nun's room. When we were confronted about it, we'd feign ignorance and suggest that perhaps one of the other orphans did it, or maybe a disgruntled Sister who had greased her own door to avoid suspicion, did it as a joke. The other children kept quiet, knowing full well that their involvements would be disclosed in the case of betrayal. The key to the Sisters' confusion was using their own misgivings against one another, sowing the seeds of mistrust and keeping them weary of one another – this is not to say that they did not suspect that I had something to do with it, as I was the first they questioned. But I was careful to choose pranks that could be perceived as accidents, for they would accuse me of the obvious ones that Sarah dealt with. I would be able to provide an alibi through other "uninvolved" orphans. I believe that was the real reason why I kept falling short in the midnight votes. As always, Sarah's popularity kept winning out, but she was never a suspect.

One night we came to a draw, and Sarah proclaimed that since she was Mother's favorite last night, that unless I did something of her choosing, that the mantle would remain with her. I was tired of losing and was desperate enough to learn her secret that it sometimes kept me up at night – so I agreed. I was bestowed a pair of metal sewing shears and sent out into the hallway with a frog lodged deep in my throat. The children quietly followed me out to make sure that I didn't back out of the deal. The prank was simple: to creep into the new Mother-Superior's room and cut off a lock of her hair. As I slowly made my way to her room, with the hand of God looming over my head, I came to realize how dead-set-against I was to the whole thing. I loved Sister Clara, and didn't want to harm her, even though she had made a complaint against me. I was positive that had it not have been for the other Sisters wickedness, that I would have been able to enjoy a positive relationship with her. But as much as I didn't want too, I simply had to claim my prize, as I was tired of falling second. I kept telling myself, as I neared her door, that after this prank I was going to be done with the game – just this one last prank and then we'd start a new one.

Much like the majority of St. Ambrose, Sister Clara's

door was unlocked and I was able to sneak easily into her chamber and slide up carefully to her bedside. Moonlight filtered in through the glass of her window, which caused her skin to shine with a seraphic aura. Around her face lay softly her midnight tresses that had always been hidden beneath her veil. She slept with barely a breath rising from her chest, and I felt that I was desecrating the dead when I snipped nearly eight inches off her longest curl. I returned triumphant, though my heart had been pounding loud enough that it should have woken all of St. Ambrose. I was named victor of the day and the smiling Sarah could do nothing but hug me, for finally losing the round. I was now Mother's favorite!

My victory didn't last long, as the next day when I approached Sarah about the secret she promised to relinquish me, she simply tossed her hair and claimed she had forgotten all about it and couldn't remember it for the life of her. I was angered at her! as if she wasn't willing to admit the defeat of last night's contest and to make matters worse, Sarah admitted to being bored with our game once again, and decided it'd just be best to end it. Though I was planning on doing the same, it only agitated me further because I did not get the choice of ending it myself – for that, the spoils of victory turned sour. There was however, one last secret that I was willing to unravel, and it was to learn where Sarah went night after night – if anything, just to spite her.

That night, when we both bedded down together and fell into rhythmic breathing, when Sarah thought I had fallen asleep, she slide outside the linen and out into St. Ambrose. I waited a few moments before following silently after. I kept to the shadows between the doors and squeezed myself into any niche that I happened to fall across while in pursuit. She drifted through the hallways and adjoining chambers like a spectre; her nighty slightly fluttering in some ethereal breeze. Sarah eventually halted at a tall oak door that was known to be locked and off-limits. But she revealed a key that she had secretly been keeping round her neck and slipped it gently into the aged lock; turning it, and entering. I was lucky that she hadn't locked it behind her and even luckier that she left it ajar a crack. I was able to slide past the heavy portal and slip stealthily in.

It was dark, but I was able to hear the sounds of Sarah's feet patting against the dusty stone floor, and so I followed it as best as I could while keeping my hand nearest the wall to ensure my way. The air was filled with a nauseating stench that seemed, regardless how I struggled, to pierce past my olfactory defenses and it stabbed repeatedly at my stomach. I reasoned, by the way in which I was walking, that I was in a hallway that stretched behind, and occasionally, between rooms in Saint Ambrose. The floor was colder than the rest of the Orphanage and made me wish that I had worn my shoes.

I stopped quickly as Sarah's footsteps halted, and I pressed hard against the wall in order to remain undetected. I held my breath, and hoped that she didn't hear the echoing of my heart inside my chest. Her footsteps came closer to me, and when I could feel her breath brushing against my face, I could have sworn she was reaching out for me like a blind crone. But then I heard her step away and onto a metal casing of sort, descending into the floor. Once it was safe to breath, I gathered my courage and continued my chase, but just then my hand fell from the wall and out into open space, until it landed softly on a metal railing, which marked the beginning of a spiraling staircase.

Once I reached the bottom step, I felt my way for the wall, and continued along its course, hoping that it'd bring me to where Sarah disappeared to. I no longer heard her, or anything for that matter, and it felt like I was being swallowed by the void that waits patiently for you before you dream. My feet rolled over abrasions, chips of something, and small stones – I became afraid that I might cut myself on some hidden piece of glass or step on a rusty nail. Then my eyes were struck to near-blindness when the sound of a striking match brought a flood of light to my face. I threw myself backwards and was lucky enough to douse a startled scream that was nearly past my lips. When my senses came-to, as it was only a brief paralysis, I found that the light was coming from a nearby break in the brick wall, just small enough to crawl through. Taking this as an opportunity to glance at my surroundings, I found that I was in, obviously, one of the forgotten segments of St. Ambrose. The metal staircase carried a slightly orange tinge that comes with rust and the floors were stained with mud and dust. Tiny pieces of mortar lay sporadically amidst the floor, and I noticed that the majority of it had fallen off the cracked ceiling. The hallway I was in, lead further than the light could reach and I became hesitant to proceed any further. I heard Sarah's voice coming from the other room, and I hastily feared that I had been discovered! but it was only a matter a seconds, as her speech sounded poised toward some other occupant in the room, that my fear grew to curiosity.

  I couldn't hear her, as her voice spoke softly and occasionally dipped in whispers. I tried to see in, but my view was blocked my all matter of boards, piles of bricks, a spade, crates, and several other items of rubble. So I was forced to squeeze myself through the gape in the wall, as much as my little frame would allot me, and crawled up to the side of a mound of bricks, and laid down so that I could only peak over the side. Sarah sat in the center of the room next to a segment of floor that had been dug up, for some reason or another, that held exposed metal pipes and a dirt floor. She had her back to me, with her head bowed to something in her lap. A copper kerosene lamp shown brightly next to her, which played her shadow against the far back wall, and she spoke in a whispered voice, "I'm sorry; I just couldn't let her know. It... it isn't right, nor the time."

  Sarah stroked the top of whatever it was that she was carrying. I thought it to be a cat that she may have found and had been keeping it down here to avoid chastisement from the other Sisters. But then –

"I did everything you told me, but you can't expect her to as well. Besides, I'm the favorite one, right? Just because she won one time, doesn't make her better."

A croaking fell into the room, echoing off the cracks in the ceilings and rippled across my spine. Sarah's voice turned as course as brick, and she shivered as the words rang out, "Play nice - give the spoils to she who won! I speak only to my favorite child."

My heart starting beating at a quicker pace as each word filled me with dread. The voice vibrated my bones, and caused the same shudder that Sarah had twitched. There was something wrong, the scent in the air, it all felt dangerously familiar to those nights my father spent howling throughout the house.

She began to cry, "You don't mean that. You love me, you said you did!" The croaking came again, and Sarah couldn't help but place her hands over her ears to snuff out the noise, "I did what you told me to do! I did it all for you! Why can't you love me, why can't I be the favorite?"

"You've been a bad girl; do what Mother tells you! Love must be earned." Sarah hissed like acid, and she stood up hold the thing in her lap like a symbol against the darkness. And I saw it! as a shadow against the wall, a twisted shade of knotted hair dangled by her hand, a round object... a head! Oh GOD! A human head! One that danced in the firelight of the damnable kerosene lamp. Sarah sobbed as she promised, "I will Mother, I will."

The croaking came again, and the horror forced my heart aflutter, which caused me to slip down the mound of bricks, but not before I saw the blazing eyes of my bedmate as she whipped her eyes in my direction. I fled in terror, ducking through the mouth in the wall and ignoring all means of silence so that I could get away. The croaking followed after, chasing me up the stairs of the rusted spiral and through the abandoned hall. It wasn't until I reached the safety of my room, surrounded by the other orphans that the noise was absorbed by the quiescence of St. Ambrose. I threw myself beneath the covers and pretended, like all those other nights when my father stared at me from my door, to be asleep. It wasn't long till Sarah came after, and I could feel her hovering over my body and staring at me with intense eyes. The fear within me wanted to scream, and run as far from her as possible, but the trick of it was to bypass it all and lay absolutely still. It must have worked, as I may have feigned something peaceful enough that she'd attribute the noise to a rat, for her to crawl into the covers next to me, cuddling close, and soon falling into dreams herself. I couldn't follow her, as I laid awake, with her arms close around me, in fear that she'd rouse to choke me if I'd betray myself by shifting. I couldn't shake the croaking, though I could no longer here it echo, it imprinted itself on my mind and bones – enough to make a lesser mind scream.

The next morning I tried to pretend that I hadn't seen anything at all and even took chores that would take me away from her. Once out of her presence I started to quiver uncontrollable, and only when I'd hear her voice or be known of her presence would my body snap back into a peaceful recluse that'd be ruled by fear and dread. Sarah would smile at me, and ask if there were any games that I thought of, that we could play together – as she'd hope to have the chance to become Mother's favorite again. And I would shake my head in a rather calm manner, return the smile, and inform her that I hadn't. I didn't understand exactly what Sarah wanted with me, and that revealing her secret would only bring me back down into that abandoned portion of St. Ambrose where I'd see the head, and hear the ghastly croaking – be driven mad, or never seen again. What prevented her from giving way to her secret, perhaps was a tiny sliver of humanity and innocence that still hid somewhere in that forsaken body of hers. I prayed, Oh God, did I pray! One of the Sisters even saw me as I knelt before the altar in the converted chapel, gossiping later that, "She might be coming around."

Then as the night slowly approached, and the dread increased with each passing moment, I looked to other things for comfort. Eventually my fingers found their way to my pocket which held the preserved lock of Sister Clara's hair. I brought it to my cheek and left the softness act as kiss, and realized that She could save me! Sister Clara would protect me with her faith, she'd protect me with her God, and dispel the demons that possessed my poor friend. Though she wouldn't believe me if I told her. I had to show her! I had to steal it! I had to let her experience that horror for herself otherwise I'd be branded for my breeding and labeled with insanity.   But that would mean having to traverse through the darkness, and exposing myself to that horrible smell and the croaking…

I knew what I had to do that night when we both laid together in our cot and once again fell to rhythmic breathing. Just like those other nights prior, Sarah lifted herself from her bed and snuck out into the hallway. I followed her, just as before, tracing that same path we took, like some recurring nightmare. She unlocked the oak door that lead to that hallway, the decrepit spiral staircase, and the rooms below. I followed carefully, allowing Sarah plenty of time to get ahead of me, while I was still able to keep notice. I covered my eyes once I reached the bottom step of the stairwell, until I heard the familiar sound of a match striking. Timing was important, as once she bent down to light the old copper lamp; I was already through the mouth in the wall. I watched her, as she uncovered a brown sack that was hidden in the opening in the floor, buried beneath the dirt. She was only able to get it to the stone floor, before I hit her in the head with the nearby shovel.   She went sprawling face-forward in the pit-like grave. I didn't take the time to see if she was still conscious. I quickly grabbed the cloth sack, my hands shaking from the thought of what I had just done, took the lamp, and left poor Sarah bleeding in the same hole the sack was pilfered from. I ran up the stairs, my heart pounding in desperation, to get to Sister Clara's room. Once I escaped through the portal of the forbidden section of St. Ambrose, the quietness of the place seemed partial to that of a tomb, and though I couldn't hear the pattering of feet behind me, I still feared the worst every time I passed a dark recess or nook. The shadows played tricks on me, like dark grimy hands reaching out of the darkness. I direly wished I could close my eyes; only to open them when within the presence of Sister Clara.

As my lungs were about to explode, I finally reached the door to Sister Clara's room. I pushed past, the noise of it startling her from her bed, causing her to cry out, "What in the world?" as I screamed for her to wake.

I set the lamp on the ground and yelled the entire story, "Sarah!.. Sister Clara... Mother! The head... Oh God the head! Don't let her get me!"

I didn't know at the time but I was crying, and shaking so profusely that one would swear I was one step from death. Sister Clara tried to comfort me, tried to get near me then backed away from the stained bag, she saw the old blood, she smelled that horrible stench. I felt as though my heart stopped completely, as I could hear something coming from inside the bag, the horrible croaking from before, soft at first, but growing by the second and getting louder – louder and louder as it made my head spin and my bones quake. I screamed, "Make it stop! Make it stop!" and thrust my hand into the bag, grabbing a clump of hair, and peeled the sack from the head like a bed of skin. As it came in the light, I beheld it in horror! It was looking directly at me, and keened my name! for the love of all that's holy, she keened my full name: Anna Rochelle Kage!

I woke, for I must have passed out from it all, on a white stretcher – I was tied down with massive straps and was being carried off by those same men from before. I could see the Sisters behind me, shaking their heads and muttering to themselves about how right they were. When I asked them about Sarah, they told me that there was an open pipe;

corroded with age; that it was sharp... she didn't make it. No one accused me of anything; honestly, no one said anything at all. I was just glad to be taken away, though sad that I wouldn't be seeing Sister Clara again. Lately, I've been discovering religion, reading up, and talking, lots of talking. The doctors are worse than the Sisters. I keep telling them the same story, but they don't believe me – but no one blames me for it. I've been thinking about getting baptized, as the whole event has left me with a new perspective. I have nightmares at night, and sometimes when I'm alone, I can hear the croaking from outside my window, and can feel it echo off my bones. I tell the doctors I want to be a nun, and that it would be nice to watch over children someday. I keep Sister Clara's hair in a safe place; I told them it was my mother's. They don't have the heart to deprive me of it. Maybe one day I'll see her again... maybe one day... but until then—who will be my mother now?

Le Château de Crane

Messieurs,

Je suis Jonathan Rupert, the head of the surgical ward at St. Jude Hospital here in the Ville de Candid in the southeastern portion of France. I write to you with explanation of my recent absences. I attest, I had not been feeling well, for I had caught a touch of pneumonia. I have been bedridden for several days, and was limited in alerting anyone of my condition. However, I am pleased to announce that my health has been restored and I fully intend to placate my previously missed appointments.

The origins of my sickness came from a series of events late one night, one for which I wish to dispose in hopes of preparation for the true purpose of this letter. I apologize if this may seem unorthodox, but I do not wish to leave anything out in case there may be some accusations against me. I will keep this as brief as I can, as I am aware of the importance of your positions and constraints of time.

My night began two hours past noon, as I would be unable to watch the sunset at the usual hour, and anyone who has been to St. Jude can complain of its lack in windows. I was occupied in the hospital's morgue, performing a routine procedure on a Monsieur J-, whom had unfortunately died under the care of a younger colleague; mysteriously and without warning. I had been entrusted with investigating the cause of the death in hopes that my colleague had not, by some twist of fate, accidentally laid a hand in his premature repose. I was confident in my confrere's abilities as a physician, and suspected that perhaps the deceased had held some form of allergic reaction to his treatment, which possibly aided in the patient's passing due to the administrations of proper medication. My personal assistant, Mademoiselle Elise Fannette, whom I've had the personal displeasure of enduring for the last nine months, aided me in the dissection. She is a beautiful girl, in her mid-twenties, and though exceedingly well mannered, I swore that she suffers from an acute form of neurosis. When I asked her to hold a tray with the sanitized instruments for the autopsy, I could not help my agitation at their consistent rattling; as her hands could never be stayed.

"Pour l'amour de Dieu—Mademoiselle Fannett, get ahold of yourself. It's not as if this man's life were in my hands!" I remarked in frustration. "If you cannot hold a simple tray, how on earth do you expect to hold a scalpel?"

She stood there, eyes sulking from yet another blunder on her part and as shy as the first day I hired her, she spoke, "Je suis désolé, Docteur Rupert." The same words that I had attributed as equivalent as a punishment from God.

As I grabbed one of the instruments in earnest, to put an end to the clamoring, I instructed the Mademoiselle to put the tray on-edge of the examination table, and then find me an undisclosed amount of pans in hopes of sectioning out Monsieur J's- organs. As she disappeared into the next room in search for the objects, I heard a foreign noise that instantly drew my attention. At first it seemed as a slight squeak, one that would issue from Mademoiselle Fannett whenever I would accidentally startle her by simple request or errand, but this was a noise that didn't come from such surprises. It sounded petite and spawned from an isolated section of darkness that the overhead bulb couldn't penetrate. I listened and could hear the near-silent fumbling of my assistant in the next room over, and pondered to myself on how difficult she managed to make each task so difficult. It wasn't until I decided to return to my work, dismissing the vile noise, to make the first incision against the cadaver, when I heard a scampering jolt towards the tray-side of the examination table and halt thereunder. I leaped backwards with weapon in hand and frantically searched for whatever had made rhythm against my ears, but feared that it had taken shelter beneath some shadow. I aimed the reflective surface of the knife in hopes of redirecting a sliver of light into the darkened void beneath the table, though unfortunately, from my angle, I couldn't gain a direct line-of-sight and had to rally upon my knees. With luck, I was able to cast a glimmer of light beneath the supporting legs. It was then that the light passed over a furred monstrosity that roused in me such a fright that caused my leg, as I scrambled to my feet, to disrupt the harmony of the tray that lay on-edge of the examination table. The instruments spilled onto the tiled floor, and in my quickened state I had managed to hit the suspended bulb, which then swung about the room, throwing light in every which place save for where it was needed the most. I swore beneath my breath, cursing the day the Almighty had created the beasts.

A few moments afterwards, as I continued to seek the furred-horror, my assistant flew into the room. Curious as to the cause of the commotion she inquired, "Sont vous d'accord le Docteur?" This proved to only grant me additional grievance, as after I halted the pendulum-like bulb, I had realized that she held not but a single dish in her hands. I became even more-so irritated at her uselessness.

"Rats!" I shouted, holding nothing but contempt.

With my assistant's return, I found no evidence that the creature was present. The rodent had retreated to whatever level of hell it had spirited from. I was able to finish the dissection without additional outworldly distraction and Monsieur J's report can be found in the permanent records cited without fault of my colleague.

I then returned to my windowless prison-of-an-office and attempted to shake the encounter. I must profess my aged hatred for the little beasts. To think of the audacity of such a thing occurring in a hospital morgue no less; to see the vile beast trespassing so freely and without fear is blatantly preposterous. Nevertheless, I assure you, I put in a swift order in the being's removal; least the hospital suffer a few partially devoured corpses.

As I eased into my chair behind my desk, I recovered a

gold-plated pocket watch that I had craftily hid within the desk drawer and sought the time. It was nearly six hours past noon, yet, as always, my work usually carried me into the late hours of the night. I read the inscription on the inside cover, "FOR 25 YEARS OF EXCEPTIONAL PERFORMANCE…" and reminisced on the very moment it had been bestowed upon me. This watch was a sign of my promotion to the head of the surgical ward - it had been a long time coming. I believe the other director had passed due to heart failure.

I recall I was growing exceptionally tired by this time, as I had developed a minor case of insomnia which kept me up late at night. In order to stave off the coming lethargy, I summoned Mademoiselle Fannett to bring my evening coffee. She brought it whilst I was in the midst of reviewing the autopsy report - the rattling of the china trumpeted her coming. Her hands trembled as she poured from the silver pot, often missing the rim of my cup, all the while I stared at her from beneath my raised eyebrow in hopes that she could read my disapproval. After depositing the correct amount of sugar and cream, she set the drenched cup upon a saucer and laid it upon my desk. I took a handkerchief from my pocket, wiped the side off and said "The proper means of pouring coffee… is to ensure that the majority of it lands within the cup and not everywhere but! Perhaps you should find a means of staying those hands of yours - that is, if you wish to be of any use to me."

She hugged the tray closer to herself, and I knew the exact words that would emit from her mouth, "Je suis désolé, Docteur Rupert."

I set the cup down in a rather harsh fashion and seized a pen and paper from my desk drawer. There upon I wrote in elegant doctoral script the name and address of a man whom I had known only through deed, a Dr. Emerson Crane. Dr. Crane was a man of notorious genius, a learned scholar of philosophy and most psychological disciplines. Though I had been known to consign my referral to clients, it was usually for only the most intense of purposes. Mademoiselle Elise Fanette was a special case.

"I do hope that you make yourself an appointment, it would better serve your continued stay here." I commented encouragingly as I handed her the psychologist's address. She looked at it particularly bewildered and might have been, at that time, a speck of dust within her eyes as they proceeded to well up in tears. She left the room without dismissal or reason thereof. I decided to be lenient on the girl, to not discipline her for her rudeness, as she was susceptible to false assumptions and feminine wiles, and beside—though presumptuous for me to claim—she happened to make the best coffee in all of Candid.

It is now that I jump ahead, as the rest of my day was filled with medical reports and unrelated surgeries that went without complication or item of note. I returned to my home quite late in the evening, nearly an hour till midnight, and now being awake, as is my custom, I fixed myself a drink. The contours of my home have relatively little to do with the basis of the story, it's nothing much to boast of, though St. Jude Hospital ensures that I do not live without comfort. I took a moment to reflect on the day's occurrences after stoking a fire in the hearth and toasting a glass of whiskey to a portrait of my beloved father, which hung above the mantle. My father was a hard working and devoted man, a physician who taught at the university in Oxford. He was brash at times, conferring with me of my inescapable future in medicine regardless of my rebellious notions of pursuing a different career. I was once disposed towards artistic endeavors; sketching, painting and the like. My mother believed that I had the hands of a pianist, but my father saw it that I should hold a scalpel instead. In the end, he proved the wiser, as after years of tyrannical lesson and lecture, I graduated at the head of my class in medicinal practices. My father couldn't have been prouder. I slipped into a comfortable armchair and finished the last drop of my drink, and no sooner did I begin to listen to the steady beats of a nearby clock, that I was finally able to solemnly fall asleep.

As I began to feel my muscles relax and my consciousness drift deeper inside myself, I was forced to an immediate sense of wakefulness by a shrewd knocking at my door. Perturbed at being roused from potential rest, I gracefully answered the door with a mild irritation.

"Do you realize the hour—" I was caught mid-sentence as I comprehended who stood beyond my threshold; a man, dressed up as one of Candid's finer courier services - letter in hand.

"Beaucoup d'apologies, Docteur Jonathan Rupert, the letter I carry has been stamped with the utmost urgencies and was told to abolish nightly courtesy to ensure its prompt deliver." He jetted the letter out towards me, in order to keep himself hidden beneath the veil of night. I took the summons with partial hesitation, but the feeling was quick to absolve when I noticed that the envelope was secured by Dr. Crane's personal seal. I nodded at the courier for his deliverance. He tipped his hat, proceeded down my steps and disappeared in the chill of the night like a phantom, without additional word or hint of compensation. I brought the letter safely into my home and broke the seal. The card within was laced in fanciful gold embroidery and the handwriting appeared welcoming. Even now the invitation's words are still fresh within my mind:

To The Illustrious Dr. Jonathan Rupert
1027 Petite route de Rosaire
Candid

I graciously address you to an opportunity of a lifetime
Tonight in humble request
To be held in your highest honor
A summons of enlightened spirit and promise
1:00

Le Château De Crane

At this moment I was perplexed as to what exactly these "promises" were, or what exactly did these "opportunities" pertain to? I was baffled at not just the summons in general, but in the overall method it had arrived. Why tonight? I checked my pocket watch and noted the time 00:17, and why so late? But I would be lying if I claimed that I was not in the least bit curious. As I had mentioned before, Dr. Emerson Crane was notorious in his field of study, good humor and genius. I reasoned that to deny him now would only serve to dissuade future invitations. It is also not an everyday occurrence that one receives a chance so opportune as to be denoted one of a lifetime. So with heavy thought, I gathered my effects, slipped the invitation into my coat pocket and walked out onto the desolate streets of Candid with nothing save the summon's words steaming upon my lips.

I was able to hail a carriage that had probably just returned from carrying a late charge. I signaled the driver with the head of my cane and waited for the vehicle to stop and the steps to descend. Clumsily, I stepped towards it and nearly sprang my ankle as I tripped over a huddled devil that squealed at me from the gutter. I turned with vengeance against the abomination and stabbed at its position with the end of my cane – just missing the vermin by a whisker.

"Pardonnez-moi Monsieur," the coachmen interceded as I watched the vile wretch flee into a steam-spewing sewer drain. "It's time that I made my next round, unless there is somewhere that you need to go, I must be off." I turned and appraised the round fellow who was pointing religiously at the carriage clock like some ancient relic, outstretched before him, reading 00:31.

He made it seem like I was fortunate; that I was lucky he had stopped at all. I was amazed at his audacity, speaking to me in such a fashion, but I was not in the mood to reprimand him for his indecency. I have prided myself on being punctual by always remaining on time, and was not about to jeopardize my morals on part of some mongrel. On the other hand, once the carriage was underway, I would have ample time to discuss with him his place in society. I gave him the address of my appointed rendezvous and paid him the allotted francs, with an additional few for added secrecy of this visitation. Though I am a man of good reputation, the people of Candid were known to draft a fiction or two about high-classed elitists engaging in shady activities during the late hours of the night. If a few francs could keep me from becoming prevalent in the local gossips, then I would be more than happy to pay it twice over.

    I didn't arrive at Le Château De Crane until nearly the turn of the first hour. The mansion was built on the far end of Candid; an isolated abode that sat atop a hill three miles from the city boundaries. It was a magnificent house that mirrored the latest evolutions of Baroque architecture, surrounded in an old cast iron fence which stretched across the boundaries of the property. I must confess that I had never been to Dr. Crane's estate, and from my initial observations it appeared out of place in comparison to the half-timbered homes of Candid's commonwealth. I admired the man for having excellent taste, and, as more of the grounds were revealed to me, I swallowed whatever doubts I may have conjured for our upcoming encounter and began to look forward to the night's affairs.

    Upon rounding the cobblestone drive, the carriage came to a complete stop. With courtesy, the coachman managed to open the carriage door with a newly found sense of propriety – a mannerism that develops with the opportunity to make additional earnings no doubt. After I descended the collapsible steps, the portly fellow took his hat off and fondled it closely to his chest in a newly found respect, "Is there anything else I may do for you, Monsieur?" I took out my pocket watch and then angled my head to meet with a luminous glow that shone from the third-story balcony windows. Noting my soon-to-be late appointment, I instructed the half-wit to meet me back here in two hours as I would need a ride home. I paid him a few extra francs with the incentive that there would be more waiting for him on a swift return. The driver thanked me and without additional word or remark, hopped back upon the carriage, took up the reigns and was carted slowly into the night.

I glanced once more to the top balcony, the only one, might I add, that was alight with occupation. Every other floor and window appeared as dark and cold as the grave. Suspended from the base of the balcony railing was a gruesome gargoyle sculpted to resemble an ashen mastiff. From its placement, it seemed that the creature was scowling down towards a fountain of Sisyphus that dominated the center of the circular drive no more than ten meters from the front doors. The fountain itself was a marvel to behold, a detailed rendition of the mythical prisoner pushing his boulder up a steep incline that slightly leveled with the mansion's second story. I was so taken in by the majesty of the place that only, once I was able to retract my senses, did I realize that I was a minute late.

Hurriedly, I bounded up the front steps, past a line of Roman columns and rapped the knocker hastily on the door. No sooner did I retract my hand did I realize, beneath the fog of my breath, that the door's knocker was comprised of a ring that hung from the mouth of yet another mastiff which was sepulchral in nature. It glared at me from the massive double-door in a sardonic grin that sent an ominous chill down my spine. The echoes of my summons dissipated through the house, and when the cold slowly crept beneath my garments causing an unpleasant horripilation, I soon began to fear that my honoring host had decided against our meeting; seeing that I had not arrived at the appointed time, and chose to retreat towards his upper bedchambers for the night. I became anxiety-ridden to think that I was being denied a proper reception due to my temporal folly. Only a few minutes, dare I say, not even a trifles worth in seconds to have fallen in such ill-repute such as this! And the only excuse or reason for this denial was the treacherous grin harbored by the iron hound. I decided, despite my forethoughts, that I would impose upon the iron guardian once again, and send yet another series of raps into the mansion foyer. Like before, my plea went unheeded.

I walked out onto the cobblestone drive and glanced once more, to ensure that my host was still awake, and contemplated the light still gleaming from the upper terrace windows. I wondered to myself, as a shrill wind caught me within its frigid touch, as to whether or not some tragic event had forestalled my host, and that he was otherwise unable, by physical restraint, or otherwise incapable of answering my calls. Fearful of some horrendous occurrence that may have befallen Dr. Crane, coupled with the dreadful thought of spending the next two hours in the cold, I resolved to dispense with pleasantries and enter upon my own violation. Returning to the front ingress, I managed to bypass the loathsome iron knocker and thus proceeded hesitantly into the dark foyer.

I was surprised at first that the door was unlocked, but after realizing that perhaps Dr. Crane had little to fear this far from the city, I reconsidered my suspicions and returned in locating my host. The house, as I had mentioned before, was dark. It had not been fitted with electrical lighting since its construction and it looked as if candlelight was the only means in which to transverse the house without stumbling blindly. Nearby, upon a small nightstand, which I was able to make out due to the moonlight that filtered in from the door, was a small kerosene lamp. Lighting it with a book of matches that laid close by, I was struck breathless as the light flooded the foyer.

Displayed before me was a collection belonging only to an old historian's dream as tapestries from older times, noble crests and archaic suits of armor lined the wall. The chamber itself held a height of about four men standing shoulder upon shoulder, reaching towards the tallest rafter. I made my way towards the back of the room where ascended brilliantly beneath a crystal chandelier, a staircase leading to the upper levels. However, once I reached the center of the floor, my ears picked up a slight disturbance that loomed ominously above me. At first it was silent, but soon, with every twitch of apprehension that my body could afford, the malady bore down with increasing volume. Above, concealed from view and upon the very rafters that hung above my head, came the little sound of fleeting paws. I lifted the kerosene lamp above my head and cast its radiance towards the upper shades. It was then, within a flash, as a monstrous shadow lurched across a cloud of incandescence, that my suspicions were confirmed and I was seized with disgust. "Vile beasts." I muttered. Yet the demonic denizens above, having heard my protests as they echoed amidst the chamber, responded by poking their wretched little snouts over a side of the cantilever, sniffed the air, and let out the most detestable retort that was ever possible of a rat, a short deplorable squeak, and whispered, "Je suis désolé."

    I took aback from the frightful dialogue, which I protest wailed forth from the vermin's callous mouth. I could not help but shake my head, believing that by some trick of echo or reverberation that caused the formation of this horror to unfold within my ears. I was awestruck, but rationalized that I had been suffering from lack of sleep and that perhaps I had imagined the entire thing. However, no matter how I reasoned it, the entire encounter left me with a loathsome feeling of dread that settled uninvitingly within my lungs.

    From this bemusement, I hastened towards the stairs, hoping that at the end of this cataclysmic nightmare there would be some form of reconcilement; a pat on the back or perhaps a glass of champagne, though as I reached the first plateau, I was able to calm my lather by gazing upon the stairwells banister. It was an elegant depiction of the war of angels, centered upon the epic battle between Michael and Lucifer. The two appeared to be forever intertwined in an eternal struggle of good versus evil, imprisoned within hardened oak. I was lulled by its beauty, so compelled in fact, that I had completely forgotten about the previous confrontation. As I continued, I perceived a painting of a giant moth that hung forebodingly above the stairwell. It partook me as a clear sign of dementia for any man to have such a ghastly creation serve as a front ornament. It chilled me, as it seemed that the charcoal lepidoptera created the darkness that surrounded it, and I could not help but feel partially drawn in by its madness. I felt cold by its presence, like some supernatural creation intended for horrendous purposes. The image recalled nightmarish dreams that I had as a child; vicious night-terrors that were never resolved, nor disillusioned by loved ones.

    I sped quickly about, intently fixated on penetrating the final floors and keeping distance from the horrid canvas. Yet it was no sooner that I took my first step that I immediately became petrified by a teeth-clenching terror that caused my heart to momentarily cease. A tearing railed my hairs to alert upon no will of my own, directed by the vaporous hand of some unseen spectre. I slowly turned to better face the ghoulish painting. There! from the very fabric of the canvas, outstretched to its furthest proportions were the forced impalements of tiny little claws reaching out towards me in abhorrent malice. I could see the blunt heads of the tiny vermin pressed against the painting's surface, glaring with their pygmy eyes and gnashing their teeth against the cloth in hopes of breaking loose from their artistic prison. It was then, oh sweet God! that my ears trembled from the scratching behind the framed work.

    I vaulted in a sweat of panic, clamoring up the stairs with a total lack of grace; with each breath I pushed through my lungs, I inhaled a strengthened dose of mania. Gripping the railing in flight, I bounded up a few additional stairs before I tripped on a hidden something, sending the metallic object crashing behind, and I plummeted upon the jagged incline. In the fumble, I managed to save the kerosene lamp but jammed my patella against the angle of the step. I gripped my knee tightly with my other hand, feeling the sanguine wound beneath my now-torn pants. I also suffered the loss of my cane, as it had snapped into two useless pieces and fell in a commotion toward the bottom steps. Fearful and without my weapon of choice, I tore my gaze back at the painting, praying that I would not be overran, that I would have a few moments to retreat to a secure room, to barricade myself against the onslaught of the freakish demons but noticed — the ghouls were gone! Not only had they fled from the painting itself but also there wasn't any particular damage or mark of any kind that would denote their previous endeavors. I checked the damage to my knee in a huddled sanctuary, seeing that the pants had torn and the skin had broke, though relieved that nothing else was disrupted. I was comforted by the thought that I would not bleed to death, especially in such unnatural surroundings.

Reminded of my wound, I sought the very object that had caused my plummet that now lay at the bottom of the stairs and brought it eye-level. The item had been a silver platter, a milk saucer to be exact, with a few portions of the residue still clung to its inner recess. The fall, apparently didn't create much of a mess, as it was apparently empty from before. It occurred to me that Dr. Emerson Crane might have purposefully left it here, perhaps as a sacrifice to appease the abominations or more likely, treated them as household pets. The more I thought about it, as I turned the saucer in my hands, I came to question Dr. Crane's overall sanity. I found myself asking if he was truly the man he was reputed to be, and whether or not I had — in good faith mind you — been sending my patients to someone who was far more touched than they. It was a horrid feeling, believing myself to have sacrificed my patients to satiate the musings of a madman.

I tarried on as I pushed myself up the remaining stairs. I reached a hallway, where, at its end, I could see a small beam of light emanating from beneath a slightly opened door. The light trail washed me with the sensation of hope and almost a literal feeling of salvation. Despite my earlier thoughts, and the disheveled condition of my clothing, I slowly made my way to the door. I exhaled the night's ventures as I attempted to swallow whatever animosity I had collected since I had arrived at Le Château De Crane, as he was my host after all, and, with a deep hardening breath of air, I brought my hand against the wooden barrier.

"Do come in." Came a calm coaxing voice. I felt relieved by its pleasantness, half dismissing my preconceived notions of Doctor Crane's character, and took the invitation with an open smile. I checked my watch and noted the time, thirteen past the hour, and then proceeded toward my humbled redemption in the next room.

The chamber initially took me by surprise. I had half-anticipated that I would be walking into Dr. Crane's bedroom, yet here before me outstretched a vast library, containing a shelf against every wall, pregnant with an allotment of books that stretched from the floor all the way to the highest reaches of the ceiling. Even the floor could not be spared from a few stacks of books that I had assumed over-spilled, or been left out due to some recent research of sorts. A fire burned brightly in the chambers hearth and filled the room with a pleasing glow and warmth. Dr. Crane stood behind a desk within the center of the room, a nice oak treasure with lion claws for legs that was surrounded by a few scattered red velvet chairs. Dr. Crane himself was more than what I was expecting; he looked roughly about 190 centimeters – a good ten above my own – an athletic trim and he held a finely sculpted physique. He looked as if he were bred of the finest of English stock, young, golden hair, and a majestic set of autumn eyes. When he looked at me, I felt as if he were looking directly into my soul, as if penetrating my skin without a feeling of violation. We looked at each other for a few short moments and afterwards, like a poetic aristocrat, he bid me welcome.

"Dr. Jonathan Rupert, I presume." His lips turned into a relaxed smile, that until now I hadn't realized had been hardened. I had hoped, that he bore me no ill. "I must apologize for not being able to greet you at the door. The help has gone home for the night and for a man of my antiquity, I tend to be easily distracted by my work." No sooner did I finally reach the front of his desk did I understand what he meant by the word "antiquity". Dr. Crane's hair had taken to the firelight cast, and instead of a beautiful blonde he actually bore a full head of gray. I could even see the wrinkles on his skin. I was shocked that I did not notice them and the shadows they cast before; already Dr. Crane was proving himself to be an accomplished magician. Nevertheless, he still held an elegant look about him, his pale hair was cut cleanly as a prince, and his eyes held that same glaze that accompanied most newborns. He was dressed in a few light pieces of clothing and a thick night robe that was tied at his waist.

We both extended our hands roughly about the same time; either we both were tied to strict tradition or we held some form of unexplainable connection that directed each other's movements. Dr. Crane was strong for his age and I was thankful that I was able to reclaim my hand in one piece.

"It's a pleasure to meet you." My host expressed most jubilantly.

"The pleasure is all mine." I retorted.

Dr. Crane opened the right drawer of his desk and pulled out a crystal bottle filled with a familiar sepia liquid. "Can I interest you in a drink? It's one of the last fine brandies that you'll ever have the chance at tasting."

"I could go for some, thank you." I said skeptically, innocently watching as he pulled out two crystal glasses and set them atop his desk, uncorked the bottle and filled each with the ambrosial nectar. He handed me a glass, took one up himself, and proposed a toast, "To your health, Doctor." There was a hidden tension in the air. I sought his eyes for some manner of deception but found them unwilling to betray his inner thoughts.

Just as we both tilted our lips to the glass and began to down the liquid, I became troubled as I watched through the prism of my glass as my host commissioned a revolver from his robe's pocket and placed it securely into the void of his desk drawer before its closing. It was a well-timed dexterous endeavor. He assumed that by taking a drink, I would close my eyes to better savor the taste, effectively hiding his treachery. The presence of the gun put me on edge, especially after I removed the glass from my lips and Dr. Crane appeared as if nothing had transpired.

Taking the glass, I swirled its contents in brooding, hoping to forgive the instrument lurking in his desk drawer and tried to disrupt the newly acquired awkwardness that I felt by giving laugh to the night's ventures, "I was beginning to believe that your home was abandoned."

"I assure you Doctor, though as dark as it may seem, it is very much alive. An old estate such as this takes a lot of effort to keep lit, I try to conserve as much as possible." I stared at him almost from a fit of hidden dread at the word "alive" and he must have noted my anxiety as to the response he gave after. "Where are my manners? You must excuse me – it has been awhile since I have last met with a guest unattended. Please do sit down." He directed me to a chair with an open palm. "I am sure if it had not been for your patient referrals that I would be unfit for social meetings. I must confess that I am a solitary man and enjoy my privacy."

Shakily I welcomed the chance to partake of a seated conversation. My knee pained me beyond imagination and the thought of a chance to relax would serve as a nurturing relief. I disposed myself of the kerosene lamp, careful to douse its flame within and set it nicely upon the ground by my chair. I unbuckled the top button of my collar as I found that I wasn't breathing well. Once my muscles sank into the pillows, I wafted a scent from my glass and commented, "Burgundy?" It was my way of extinguishing the tension.

"Close. It's German. I had it scoured from the cellar a few nights ago. It's an interesting brand. Unfortunately the estate responsible for the mixture fell in finances and is no longer in production. It's too bad. I have acquired a strong taste for it. As a French philosopher once said, 'C'est la vie'. When one grows older, one has a harder time accepting change especially when it comes to choice favorites... Don't you agree, Doctor?" Dr. Crane took the bottle of Brandywine and a collection of papers with him around his desk as he sat in the seat directly across from me.

"Please, call me Jonathan." I mentioned while noting the suspicious papers within his hand.

"Of course, I was wondering if you were willing to dispense with formalities. I personally do not care for them much, especially between reputable colleagues such as us. I don't contend well with my initial name so please..." he paused, "Call me, Crane." I nodded my head in approval before my host continued, "I haven't had the opportunity to invite you during optimal hours due to your tendencies to work late. Being a physician of my own pursuits, I can relate. I am glad that we are able to pilfer such a time as tonight for a meeting."

"I agree." No sooner were these words spoken, did my ears pick up a salient scratching noise hidden amidst the sea of stacked books. My hairs took towards the ceiling in a reminding caution that a rogue rodent might have scurried into the room. My eyes darted towards the door that I had entered from and noticed with a perturbed sense of self-loathing that I had left it slightly open, enough for a small assassin to squeeze through. My recklessness now proved to be my tormentor. As my head then ached with the increased palpitation of my heart, I returned my attention back to Crane in hopes he hadn't notice my concern, "Do you plan to sketch me?" I asked in good humor in order to starve off any accusations against my fullest attention, while nodding towards the papers he held in his hands.

"Oh, these?" He lifted them closer to his wrinkled face as if recognizing them for the first time. "I like to keep parchment in front of me, in hopes of capturing any moment of revelation. Pay them no mind. When one becomes as old as I, one tends to write everything down least one should forget shortly after." Crane set the papers on the desk nearest him. "I've heard a lot about you Jonathan, you are the splitting image of your father." He cupped his hands together and I wondered if he was a religious man or about to unfold some hidden conspiracy.

"You knew my father?" I asked while notably perturbed. I did not transverse this asylum to speak about my father.

"Oh yes, I attended one of his lectures whilst I was visiting Oxford. He had an insurmountable amount of insight into human anatomy, quite the learned man if I remember correctly. I am a bit surprised to see that you did not follow his path as a scholar." Crane leaned backwards into the seat cushions and took a drink from his glass. His furry eyebrows performed a shrewd ballet as the flavor touched his tongue.

"Well, my father was far more interested in seeing me through a doctorate in medicine than complimenting my achievements by a position in the college. We've had our differences in the past and Candid needed a surgeon. The rest, I assume, speaks for itself."

"I see." Dr. Crane narrowed his eyes as if doing so would pry information from my mind, "If I may be so bold, how do you feel about that?"

"Personal feelings are a bit irrelevant don't you agree, Crane? We are talking about my father, are we not?" I did not despise my father for denying me a future at Oxford, nor did I feel abhorrent towards him in any fashion for directing me towards Candid.

Crane leaned forward with an almost overpowering mysticism, "Are we?"

I caught a shadow flashing against one of the bookshelves behind Crane, as he tried to ponder some obtuse riddle. At this point, I was too distracted to be concerned at what Crane may have been hinting at. The beast was now canvassing the room for some leftover morsel no doubt, scrounging for a shadow of food in hopes of satiating its eternal appetite for just a few seconds more. My spine tinged in apprehension, and I could feel the creature's shadow passing over me as I desperately sought the monster amidst the maze of literature.

I do not know how long Crane had been staring at me, but I managed to catch him leaning back into his chair before he felt complacent to speak again, "Do you have any regrets, Jonathan?"

I felt a bead of sweat collect upon my forehead and then run down the side of my face. I could feel the vile devil making its way amidst the aisles of books, searching the loose pages with its grotesque nose, and feeling its way with haunting whiskers. I shuddered at the thought of such a thing sharing the same air as I, mixing its putrid essence amidst two intellectual giants. It wasn't until I heard a low thunder in Crane's throat that I realized he was watching me, intently - more so than I was comfortable with.

"Regrets? Don't be naive. Granted I was a bit rebellious as a child, but I managed to secure an education and become the head of the surgical ward here in Candid. I am a knowledgeable man. I live in comfort. What more can a man ask for?"

Dr. Crane stroked his chin in contemplation, "Yes, what more could a man ask for?"

His line of questioning began to make me angry. I wondered whether Dr. Crane had called me to his home in order to "honor" me, as his summons had so entailed, or if this was more of a means of profiling me or meant as a form of outlandish intimidation. Yet, I pondered the question—if only to humor him.

"Perhaps a more competent assistant." I smirked while fondling the glass' rim.

"Yes - the wondrous Mademoiselle Fannett." I seemed to have struck a chord. "I was able to make her acquaintance a month ago, charming young girl, makes wonderful coffee; perhaps you're not giving her the credit that is due."

Then I knew. My hopes of a night filled with philosophy and enlightening conversation was dashed to tiny shards. The truth of the summons became clear. Crane's purpose here was not to engage in a delightful dialogue. Instead, he was to act as a mediator, someone to interject on behalf of Mademoiselle Fanette; to bully me into accepting her blunderings as something natural. A month ago? I thought. I laughed to myself, as Crane continued to speak about his observations of her. I chuckled at the irony of it all, having given Mademoiselle Fanette Dr. Crane's home address and they having already met. I wondered what kind of a relationship they carried? Was it professional? Were they friends? Lovers? I heard Crane between my thoughts, carrying on about her general shyness and overall nervousness caused by her social inadequacies and desires to be "liked" by others. I became nauseated by his persistence in speaking of her, my incompetent assistant, as if she were a saint. I had uncovered the man's rouse and I would not be as easily moved.

Immediately, before I could bring any of my thoughts to action, there was a sharp pain in my left knee. I looked somberly down towards my patella, the motion felt like I was in a dream-like state as everything else appeared to blur, yet my head clear was enough to see the trepidation that would soon overtake me. Sitting atop my knee, like some ghoul, was the nightmarish rodent licking and gnawing at my open wound, pressing its horrendous snout through my pant leg and into the blood soaked laceration. I pulled to a shriek of wraithlike proportions and leaped to standing on the velvet chair; coveting the wound from the creature's sadistic tortures. Crane took aback, alarmed at my outburst.

I garnished him a feral look of ravaged hatred and spoke as if inspired by the divine, "Damn you, Crane! Be damned by your infernal questioning! Your home is infested monsieur! Infested with your senile convictions and contemplations, allowing your door to be opened to these squalor rodents! How freely you sit there and ponder as a sphinx and fall victim to the whims of degradation. This is your home and you are of stature, yet you tolerate these creatures, the same that seize it all from you! Damn you, Crane, damn you and these rats!" I was out of breath, my fists were shaking in a rage that I had never felt since many arguments past with my father. I felt humiliated, outraged and above all else deceived by the very nature of the night's occurrences. I was willing to ignore the previous slights from before, fully intending to ascribe the past as night phantoms or the product of a tired mind, but this! This was far beyond redemption. I was to sit here and be eaten alive, consumed! beneath the roof of Crane's estate. This was too much to bear!

Dr. Emerson Crane, the greater man, the man who has been compared twice over to the genius of Caesar and ambitions of Alexander, a man of all men in his field, simply stared perplexed at my statement. He held onto my words as though they bore an incognita of their own. He shuffled his hands to each side of his chin, smiled at my disposition and announced with suppressed laughter, "There are no rats here doctor, I assure you."

"No rats!" I laughed with a laugh accustomed to when faced in a situation where there was nothing to do but laugh. "No rats?" I have seen these rats of yours! They are everywhere! Ever since I stepped foot within this Chateau – this death! have I witnessed the presence of these devils! Do not pretend that they do not exist! Just a moment ago one of those beasts attacked my knee, I've heard them upon your rafters, clawing behind your paintings, and frolicking amongst your books. They are nesting, dear sir! Nesting in your home and keeping stealth about it!"

My forehead perspired and the sweat from my anger boiled against my skin. I took greater intakes of breath, to stave off the feelings of anger. My fists were clenched tightly by my side as my host continued to look at my strangely. I glared at him with hostility as he slowly stood and pulled a separate glass from his desk drawer, filling it with the same poison as before. He held it out to me and motioned with his head for me to follow.

In an attempt to subside my feelings of aggression, he indulged me in a brisk walk out onto the stone balcony, through a pair of glass-paned doors, and into the piercing cold night air. It felt good against my pores, retracting my sentiments of hatred. From atop the terrace, I could see the lights of the city, and especially those surrounding the Saint Jude Hospital. It was then that I realized how exhausted I truly was; perhaps from most of the night's ventures, perhaps from the lack of sleep within the past few years, but tired of all things in general. In a short passing, I lost all form of spite towards my aged companion and focused my frustrations on the thought of another tomorrow. I walked up to the railing and attempted to release the remaining quivers. It was not long after that my host begged a calming question, "Is everything all right, Jonathan?"

"The night has not been a pleasant one, so please forgive me if I had reacted too harshly."

"I suppose there was adequate reason for it. I want to ask you a question Jonathan, and I do not mean to cause you any distress by asking, but are you happy with your life?"

I pivoted slightly in his direction to keep my words from the prying ears of Candid. I searched the man's expressions in an attempt to seize any hidden intentions. "What do you mean?" I asked with suspicion.

"Are you happy?"

"What form of query is that?" There was a little extra bile mixed between my words.

"I am not here to antagonize you. It's a question, nothing more." My host stood his ground.

"I'm well off."

He appeared confused, "Meaning...?"

"Meaning – I am well provided for. My practice! Candid! My position as the head of the surgical ward, everything I have is well provided for!"

"I believe that I am beginning to understand now." Crane walked closer to me. We were now no more than an arms length apart, where as before he kept to the door in hopes of seeing my mood refreshed. "I am beginning to see that things have not gone the way that you had wanted."

I took a step back and gave him an inquisitive look, "What are you talking about?"

"I'm talking about your mannerisms, your reactions to Mademoiselle Fannett, your defensiveness whenever I mentioned your father, everything seems to be pointing to the fact that you are unhappy with the way you view your life."

My temples throbbed. The pain was indescribable. I threw my hands up to massage my fingers into the side of my skull in an attempt to alleviate the pressure. I managed to muster, "I don't think you know what you're talking about. My life is fine."

"Oh – but I think I do, Jonathan. Why else would you seek me out in the middle of the night if there wasn't something distressing you, keeping you from your sleep?"

"What...?" My confusion only added to the pain. An explosion then ripped my attention from the man in front of me, and diverted it back towards the room we had once occupied. I stared with utter horror as the center of the floor, the very space where we had been sitting, erupted with the expulsions of hundreds of rats! My lungs sunk in terror as I became paralyzed with fear. The horde of rats swarmed against the glass wall, pushing against the door, climbing atop one another in a bestial fury. Each one scraped at the glass and pressed their noses against the pane. I screamed in my mind as my host tried to rationalize his analysis, but I could not comprehend his words. The glass cracked beneath the pressure and it streaked against the barrier like a ghostly hand. Crane looked at me in a queer fashion and his face was replaced with a furred muzzle, "Sont vous d'accord?"

The glass collapsed in a shower of tiny shards and the rats swept across the balcony in a murderous frenzy, squeaking and calling out in an ear-piercing sonance. They pushed forward like winged spirits, haunting the skies with their death-cries, all in hopes of feasting upon my flesh! I bellowed a scream that echoed toward the far city of Candid as the vermin nearly came against me. My feet instinctively leapt backwards, causing my body to slam into the balcony's railing, and my vision swiveled as I tumbled helplessly over.

Frantically I grabbed at the fleeting stone and my arms jolted as I managed to catch hold of the haunting mastiff. My descent halted, though almost dislocating my arms in the process. My pocket watch slipped from my person and dashed itself onto rubble at the feet of Sisyphus twenty feet below. I lifted my head toward a cry of mercy above me to see my host's saintly face returned to normal.

"Jonathan! Quickly! Give me your hand!" He yelled as he stretched his palm towards me.

I reached to indulge my sense of self-preservation but slipped! I reconnected to the ashen gargoyle, as the rats emerged from atop the balcony's railing. I shook my head, acknowledging my ill-begotten fate, "No I can't! The rats, Crane! Don't you see the rats?"

He looked about him in a misplaced bewilderment and retorted, "Jonathan – listen to me! There are no rats! These things that you are seeing aren't real. They are your inner demons, perhaps your judges as well. I believe there is a war going on inside you, between doing what you desire to do and that what you had been forced to accept. You have to choose to live a life that was designed for you, or set off and discover the one that you were meant for. Listen to what your heart is trying to tell you, do not let yourself fall to ruin. You have to make a choice! Now give me your hand!"

I stared at the vigilant beasts, feeling the strain of my body swaying against the emptiness below, and I tried to suppress the fear that lay within me. I could feel them in my mind, I could feel them scraping against the walls of my skull, mimicking Crane's word, repeating them in a grim melody, like a choir of specters chanting, Choose! Choose! Choose! I shut my eyes to gather strength, to force them from my vision, to force them from my mind. My muscles wavered and it was then that I felt myself beginning to slip. I reached out with my hand, catching my host's and was dragged harmfully up the side of the balcony.

Before long I found myself sprawled upon the frigid stone floor of the third story balcony. I panted, not from being out of breath, but from out of fear, as my heart palpitated in a succession of beats far grander, far faster than I had ever felt before. I coughed and from the swallow that came after, I tasted iron as a stream of blood issued from my nose. Still upon my hands and knees, with my savior only a dash to the side, I pulled a handkerchief from my pocket and brought it securely to my nostrils. I looked about the premises, nodding in a gleeful, yet fatigued nod in acknowledgement that my tormentors had fled. I cast a look in my host's direction. He couldn't help but smile, and it was that smile that made me ask, "Is this what you meant by 'an opportunity of a lifetime' Crane?"

My host simply exhaled from his smile, "An opportunity of a lifetime? What do you mean?"

"Don't be coy, I am talking about the invitation that you had sent earlier this evening." I believed that my savior was playing with me.

"I don't know what you're talking about. You came

upon your own accord."

He was playing with me. "The summons, Crane, which you bid be delivered to me by messenger at approximately seventeen minutes after midnight."

Crane softened his smile almost to fit that of a frown, "I promise you I sent no such summons. In fact, I wasn't sure of whom it was stalking about my house so late at night. I had armed myself in case you had intended harm. You noted this, did you not?"

"I did." I was vexed. I could not fathom whom it had been that sent the letter. "But, it had your seal upon it... the messenger... he claimed he was told to 'abolish nightly courtesy'. I have it upon my person and –" I reached shakily into my pocket and found it empty. "I could have sworn I kept it with me, perhaps it's still at my home. But I swear to you I–"

"I'm sure it's not there, Jonathan. The mind can be a powerful instrument, capable of many beauties, but also the maker of phantasms. You have a strong and resilient soul. Perhaps... perhaps this is your chance to rediscover what it is that you have been ignoring for many years. Your soul seems to whisper its secrets to you, I am sure in time you will find what it is that you wish to pursue."

I stared at him for the longest time, digesting the night's events, his words, and questioned everything that had transpired. Was I a man locked away from his true purpose? By surrendering to my father, did I surrender a portion of my soul as well? Or had all this been a rouse, a trick played upon me by the man who sat across from me, the revered Dr. Emerson Crane? As I gathered my breath, along with my wits, I could not help but cast my eyes once more towards the city of Candid, realizing my utter despise and feelings of resentment. How could I meet tomorrow if I did not understand today?

We spent the rest of the hour attempting to meet my previous expectations. We talked about philosophy, art, history, music and love. At no time was the previous encounter mentioned, and subjects relating to my father or my work had been purposefully avoided. It was the least he could do after such a tragic affair, and the least I could do to indulge him for my intrusion. But as the hour soon closed, I found myself at base of Sisyphus about to step into the carriage and embark on what I would hope to be a quiet journey home.

Crane stood at his porch, his front door half cracked to allow the light of the kerosene lamp to filter into the night. He watched me with a sincere glow in his eyes. I nodded to him. Then, just as I was about to disappear into the coach, I noticed a strange something glistening from the light cast by my driver's lamp. I stooped to inspect it, and found the devastated remains of my pocket watch, the hands stopped, fused to the dial at exactly 1:24. I took the thing, merely as a memento, and placed it securely within my pocket. I tarried and took one last glance round the grounds, knowing that I would never again set foot within Le Château De Crane again. As I exhaled, I said my goodbyes a second time and then, without fear or regret, entered the carriage and slapped its side from out the open window to inspire my driver home.

I watched from the back window of the coach as Crane waved to me in his night robes. And it occurred to me that perhaps the night was his doings after all, that his sick demented mind reveled in other's torment and suffering; the ultimate trickster, his genius, finally revealed. But all was lost to me when I heard his voice call into the night, a single name of Cerberus! And moments later, from out of some darkened shadow stalked the silhouette of some beautiful feline that curled affectionately about Crane's legs. As they slowly shrank into the distance, I saw them disappear within. Crane stuck his head out one last time, and I could have sworn that from beneath the radiance of the kerosene lamp his withered features retracted in the light and he looked ages youthful again. I could tell, even after he blew out the lamp, and after he shut out the night, that he was smiling to himself due to some hidden humor.

And so it is with a lightened heart that I write to you of these events, to accommodate any questions pertaining to my humbled resignation from St. Jude Hospital. Though I am sure that my services will be missed, I will be presumptuous in concluding that I cannot be blamed. As for my personal assistant, the Mademoiselle Elise Fanette - she has proven to me in the past few weeks as someone of immense character and talent. She was kind enough to help me through my sickness and she was also a woman of fine consul during my time of need. She has most graciously accepted my tutorage and I cannot speak higher of her professionalism and talent. Together we plan to return to England, in hopes of following Dr. Crane's professional advice. I hope that it is there I may be able to return to some previously imagined state of happiness and pursue it to the best of my abilities. I hold many wishes for your future success.

Time has made rodents of us all. It's my turn to rise above them and seek a more enlightened purpose.

-Dr. Jonathan Rupert, 1894

Tales of Enoch
The Watchers

"And it came to pass when the children of men had multiplied that in those days were born unto them beautiful and comely daughters. And the angels, the children of the heaven, saw and lusted after them, and said to one another: 'Come, let us choose us wives from among the children of men...'"
(The Book of Enoch the Prophet 6:1-2)

Somewhere in the great desert of man, where the ash of volcanic eruptions has stained the once green landscape, a luminous structure jets out of the baked earth. It is here, several miles from the last communication pylon, far from the glorious and sole city of humanity – Enoch, lies the last breath of a pair of explorers whose blood mixes at the base of the structure; the ground now reminiscent of the corroded soils of Mars.

Their features are darkened by the shadow of the monstrosity, still showing the awe and wonderment they held before succumbing to the calling of death. Curious beings, they were drawn to it due to its monolithic proportion, now left to nothing more than the contemplations of oblivion. It is neither age nor disease that struck them down into the soot, but by charges of plasma scored deep into their spines from the barrel of a gun, they are unaware of the dangers hidden in the dunes. And as their expressions fall into the relaxed face of entropy, their bodies are slowly dragged through the sand and deposited someplace hidden. It is there in the unknown, where their story will be laid to waste, claimed by the acidic rains and dust storms that happen occasionally by.

The truck shakes as it speeds down the artery, striking each pothole as if it were a necessity for its existence. One would think that the Enoch Road Recyclers could afford a decent pair of shocks on this old refurbished Ford, but apparently the ERR didn't want to waste the twenty-eight pounds of metal. At one time or another, someone would have considered this hunk of junk an antique, but now it's nothing more than a beater for transporting contractors such as myself.

I try my luck with my ArmLet-Computer and attempt to tune into the Line where I last left off on my song list. Over two thousand years of music and the ALC refuses to get past the local channel – static. The occasional burp of random notes, clicks and buzzing that manages to break out of the hissing, reminds me of that Tycho-Filth crap that's been so popular lately. I tap at the screen in hopes that the motions would bring some life to it, but my driver only affirms my suspicions.

"Too far from the pylons, Mr. Burbanks. Nothing but open territory and a waste-filled sky to keep you company."

My truck-mate is a man of pale complexion, dark shaggy brown hair, big muscles, and impeccable hygiene. It's only once in awhile, when someone returns after a prolonged stay in the desert, that they show signs of the decay. Some quack-pot scientist thought it had something to do with solar radiation, mineral radiation, or something that was radiated but the truth of the matter is no one knows how one gets it. It's the same explanation for why the plants won't grow or most mined ores are bad, or why the sky is perpetually blighted with ash. They told us it was supposed to be over in a couple of years but goddamn, since the cataclysm everything's gone to shit. Some say that mankind's cursed and the world right along with it. Funny what one seven mile in diameter asteroid can do. All I want is a decent song to make existence pass smoother. I sigh partially annoyed.

"I've never been this far out." I reply. "This better be

something important. I'd hate to come all this way just to find out it's made of plastic. You know how people are with dumping their trash."

"Trust me, Mr. Burbanks, this isn't some minor errand." He has a bounce in his voice which makes me believe he's struggling to withhold his excitement. It's my twenty-fifth run. They're all the same.

I try to seem interested by refusing to look up from my ALC. "Well, what is it then?"

"I'm under strict orders from Mr. Fontaine not to say anything about it; something about not attracting any attention; keeping the treasure seekers out. I'd hate to lose our share of the find."

"The law clearly states that anything found beyond the fringes of Enoch is considered property of whomever is first to discover it." I quote verbatim from a line of memorized script. "Besides, there isn't anyone here but me."

"Yea, but the law doesn't hold past the boundaries of the city. Times are difficult, and in difficult times people become desperate. I've seen men kill each other over an aluminum can. Once can't be too careful. We're just humble road recyclers." He chuckles lightly to himself. "Orders are orders." He forwards a smirk.

Fine, let him keep his secret. I shut down my ALC to conserve power and turn my head relatively unconcerned from my overly-paranoid companion. "Whatever you say…" I pause. "What was your name again?"

"Alvin, Sir. Alvin Stencil."

The truck stops five hours past the last checkpoint. Alvin's mind seems aimed at one thing and he isn't about to tell me his target. Why is it that whenever road-scrappers dig something up they always have to rush to get an appraiser? Hours, sometimes days, of work are lost - depending upon how far they're out - just so someone can estimate the amount of metal, so that the dividends can be paid out and work can resume. I guess out here it's every man for himself.

Their camp is comprised of a couple pavilions, a few band-aid trucks and haulers. The 1975 Ford I'm riding in looks the most complete. I debate whether they a wanted to impress me or if it was the only vehicle that could make the trip. The largest item of their establishment is a three-story wreck on treads called the Mastodon, accompanied by the Enoch Road Recyclers Inc.'s slogan, "Tearing down bridges to build new ones," right beneath its name and serial numbers. The whole thing should be melted down and put out of its misery.

As soon as I step out of the truck, Alvin hands me a ventilator mask.

"Environment shots only go so far. I'm not sure how the weather will be, hopefully low winds, but as I said before you can't be too careful. Once you get a face full of ash you'll thank me. Breathing out here is difficult without the comforts of the city's oscillators, so we make do with what we have. The temperature will drop as soon as the evening hits. We have some extra coats, if you'll need one."

"Thanks, Alvin." I get right to business. I hate being out here. "Now where's this Mr. Fontaine you spoke about earlier?"

"Follow me." And he proceeds to lead me in the direction of a larger tent, a couple hundred yards from a portion of torn up road, demolisher and similar equipment.

As my eyes scan over the rubble I can't help but ask, "Just what exactly do you get out of those rocks anyway?"

"Mostly? We just crush it up and recycle the aggregates: stone, gravel, sand, slag, dust, powder and occasionally glass. But it's the under-woven metal that we're really after. The rest is just bonus."

"Where is everyone?"

"Inside the Mastodon on lockdown," Alvin doesn't miss a step. "Ulrich wanted to keep tabs on everyone's whereabouts until you would arrive for the appraisal. Keeps everything fair, with no one breaking off chunks for themselves. Those who are lucky enough to have responsibilities outside of crumbling are around here somewhere, keeping out of sight. It's the new hires we worry about."

"You mean people actually live in that trash heap?" I ask while casting a backwards glance toward the eighty-foot long titan.

Alvin stops mid-stride and turns seriously. "All due respects, Mr. Burbanks, but the Mastodon is not garbage! She's seen more roads, dust storms and taken far greater share of acid rain than anything I've ever encountered. She's low maintenance and she gets the job done."

By the sound of his voice, one would think that I insulted his child. "Point earned." I figure it's best to change the conversation. "So what's she run, 150… 151 tons?"

"Very good, Mr. Burbanks, 151." His mood lifts exponentially.

"She'd make a fine ship one day." I say while thinking out loud.

"She sure will, once business dries up, but that won't be in my lifetime." He pulls back a flap of plastic covered canvas once we've reached the largest tent. "In here, Sir."

A gruff voice calls out from farther inside. "It's about time that damn surveyor showed up."

Alvin gives me a reassuring nod. "I've got the truck to tend to."

I return the same, before stepping inside the structure. The flap closes snuggly behind me.

The tent is secured by a series of plastic support beams, wrenches and ropes. Scattered throughout are plastic tables filled with an assortment of varying equipment: scanning tools, brushes, old fashion filter screens and other outdated antiques. Set atop a circular pedestal in the center of the room is a 17th-century armillary sphere. I wonder how a bunch of dirt-movers got their hands on it. It's made mostly of copper, some stainless steel, roughly 18 pounds, I'm sure it'd make the beginnings of a pilot's console. Maybe that's why they're storing it.

Mr. Fontaine is just a handshake away.

"Good to finally meet you in person, Mr. Burbanks. I've heard numerous things from a couple of the other teams working the southwest sector. You come highly recommended. I'm Ulrich Fontaine, head security of this rabble." He squeezes my hand in a good healthy shake.

He is a muscular man, though nothing in comparison to Alvin Stencil, stout, with a couple of scars running across his right cheek. He looks like he's seen his fair share of roads. He carries a Styllus-251 pulse pistol in a holster at his side, expensive - 3.6 lbs, non-recyclable - not the type you'd want to upset.

"My reputation is based directly on my availability and willingness to travel. Though I will admit, I was a little hesitant to venture beyond the fringes of Enoch." I return with the squeeze of his hand.

Ulrich chuckles from his gut. "Afraid the decay'll get ya?"

I tap the black screen of my ArmLet-Computer. "I get bored easily."

"Well I don't expect to take too much of your time. We'll swing you right over and you can give us the estimate. Once we get it all straightened out, I'll radio a few people, arrange some deals and you'll get your due once the pilots drop in - couple days, tops."

"Super."

"You folks still taking credits?"

"Unfortunately." I squeeze between my teeth. There are laws for appraisers against taking metal as payment.

"Well, Callaghan's holding down the fort as we speak – sure knows how to handle things. A bit saucy, if you know what I mean..." And before I'm able to make any conclusions Ulrich slaps my chest with the back of his hand. "Come on,

Alvin's got the truck warmed up for us. You're going to love it."

I can hardly contain my glee as I rub the pain out my breast while following wearily behind. It seems that everyone who's seen this thing is ecstatic as all hell.

I wonder whether they'd be willing to accept the armillary sphere as a partial trade. Enough metal and I can buy a ticket off this rock. It's too bad that I can't get in on whatever they've found, conflict of interest and all. In my opinion, it's always the appraiser who gets screwed. I'd have to settle for the standard fee and find a mineral dealer later on at a inflated price. Everyone hordes metal now a'days.

I make my way to the passenger seat whilst Alvin hitches a ride in the back trailer and covers his face with a ventilator. My new chauffeur throws the Ford into first gear before I've even begun to get settled in. I'm jostled forward as I hear the gears stripping.

"Sorry about the ride," Ulrich offers once he clears open ground. "I can hardly contain myself."

Great, you too huh? I think to myself while fumbling for the seat belt.

My driver removes his hands from the wheel and steers with his knees just long enough for him to pull out a half-smoked cigar from his pocket and light it with a match. Smoke spews from his lips before he returns his hands. The Ford rattles as it passes over the uneven terrain at a good ninety miles-per-hour.

He raises his voice in order to shout over the turmoil of the truck. "I keep things comfy around here and that haul we stumbled across is going to mean trouble if we let it sit for too long, not to mention all the work that's been lost."

"How long have you been down?" I yell.

"Near twenty-four hours now. I've been worried that one of the other teams has taken an interest in our production loss. Everyone keeps close tabs on one another."

"One would think it a good thing."

A sly smile reaches round his face. "One would think."

We reach the site in less than a half-hour. I can see pieces of flat-beams jetting out of the cracked earth, as black as asphalt; relay antennas; broken subsections, with parts of its interior exposed; all connected via a buckled hull, for the most part still intact, and partially buried in the dirt; all nearly 40 feet in height, spread out across a span of at least 100 feet in length.

My jaw must have dropped as Ulrich retorts to my surprise, "You guessed it, Chief!"

It's a ship! The bastards found the remains of a ship! I can't believe it. Yet its majesty and awe is ripped from me when I hear the unsnapping of my driver's holster.

"Looks like we might have some company after all..." He says, as he motions toward the base of the windshield.

Ahead of us, beneath the shadow of the colossus, sits a metallic beast, dual treads for mobility and at least one-and-a-half or maybe two inches of armor. I recognize it from one of the many old World War movies I viewed from the Line's archives. It has a mount for a machinegun, thankfully missing - must have been confiscated by Enoch officials at some point. It smells of 11 tons, give or take a little – I need to see the insides to be sure. What riles Fontaine is the four men standing a few feet from their M113 transport, petrified in place by the occupant of a portable 20 foot tower nearly 120 yards off. The lone figure keeps them in place by the barrel of his rifle. They don't appear to be armed.

The men notice the truck and shift nervously, all save one who I guess to be their leader. He waves at us to reinforce an illusion that he belongs here. My stomach churns, a bit of discomfort warning me that nothing good can come from this encounter.

"There's a box beneath your seat." My driver says as he checks his pistol's battery. "Take what's inside and put it in your pocket." His face is dead sober.

I reach beneath my seat, pull out the heavy wooden case and find waiting inside a 38 special.

"I thought projectile weapons were outlawed?" I ask with particular disdain toward the nickel-plated gun.

Ulrich opens his door with a dooming creak. "Law only applies to where it can be enforced. I'm just looking out for your well being. I'd take it, if I were you. It might just save your life." With that, he swings his boots out onto the grit of the ash colored earth, leaving me to my decision. I make a quick one, not wanting to miss much and pocket the weapon, all 1.5 pounds of it. And here I was worried about being bored.

I meet up with Alvin who stalks slowly behind, carrying a tire iron he pilfered from the back of the truck. I keep my eyes on the sniper atop the lone tower. The figure doesn't move, too devoted in keeping them in place. It's impossible to read what he's thinking, as he's obscured from head to foot in leather, cloth and a visor.

I catch the light hum that issues from a pulse-energy weapon once it's turned on, and I look cautiously between Ulrich and the men up ahead. I cannot describe to you the unparalleled shift between enthusiasm and the soberly-disguised apprehension that has taken place in the past few minutes. The reality of it sets in when I notice the scoring left by a pulse discharge on one of the men's dusters nearest his heart. The sniper must have fired a low-charge warning. He's lucky it didn't induce a heart attack.

Ulrich is the first to speak.

"Good afternoon gentlemen, is there something that I can do for you?"

The calm man, black hair, dark eyes, takes the address as if it hadn't been riddled with misgivings. "You'll have to forgive the trespass. I am Raus. I was not aware that this miscellany had been claimed. If you take no offense in me asking, what is your associating party, Sir?" He is of a slim build, toned, though a lot thinner than those behind him. His eyes are sunken, his lips are gray, and he flashes his black teeth in a wide serpentine grin – sure signs of the decay.

"Division 16 of the ERR and yes, this has already been seized under statute 9 of the Enoch Salvage Law. Best you boys just head out if you want to avoid any trouble."

"Division 16? We're from Division 4, like brothers in the field. I hope you don't mind our intrusiveness and take foul from our presence." He licks his dry cracked lips before continuing, "I assure you of our good intentions. We were merely marveling at the curiosity before we were fired upon by your assassin. It wasn't very neighborly."

"You know better than to stick your nose into other people's claims." Ulrich spouts already annoyed. "You brought that stun onto yourselves. Now get into your vehicle and vacate the premises. Everything in a one-thousand foot radius is ours and I'd hate to see your filth affect the appraisal."

Raus bares his teeth like a hissing cat, emphasizing those infectious gums, but as his men start to leave until he thrusts out his hand to stall them.

"And if we refuse?"

Ulrich pulls his pistol out of its holster but keeps it low. "No more warning shots."

"Fair enough, I just wanted to be sure where we stand." He motions to his men and they follow him back to the transport. As the last man disappears into the vehicle, Raus looks about him one last time and chuckles while saying, "Extra territorium jus dicenti impune non paretur," before vanishing himself.

I keep my hand gripped tightly around the handle of the gun, even after their engine starts and the treads push themselves in reverse. It isn't until they're completely gone that my stomach is able to relax.

"What did he just say?" I ask as I stare into their settling dust cloud.

"Don't worry about it." Alvin says with a prophetic

glare toward the horizon, "Just something to make him feel better."

Ulrich doesn't look so sure.

The sniper from atop the tower has already touched ground. With his rifle slung over his shoulder, the figure makes his way towards us, slowly unbuckling his head gear, and stripping off the ventilator he had hidden amidst the rest of his equipment. Then I realize that beneath all the bulky fittings is a red-dye number, short hair, copper eyes, beautiful lips —

"Bout time you fucking showed up. I was about ready to pop some heads and I'm not referring to those junk-rats!" He had all the graces of rustic society. Just one thing, the sniper is a woman. Callaghan, I presume.

"You sure stirred up a whole lot of something up there, Boss." Ulrich tosses her an unopened pack of Rich or for Poor cigarettes from his coat pocket.

It doesn't take her long to tear into it with her finger nails and light one up for good measure. She inhales the smoke deeply and exhales as if she'd been suffocating.

"The bastards got what they deserved. I kept asking for an excuse, but they played it smart and stayed put. You'd think the scouting beacons would have dissuaded them. Everyone's looking for a easy payoff." She sucks the ash all the way to the filter in less than a minute, throws it in the dirt, and pulls out another – this one to savor. "Mandy never showed up for her shift. I'm pulling twelve hours."

He seems unconcerned, "Boss, this is Harmon Burbanks, the appraiser. He's here to take a look whenever you're up to it."

She squats down and eyes the terrain. "This is more than a two man crew and I can't haunt this forever. We're going to have to put some faith in the boys not to scuttle outta here with their pockets lined. I think it'd be better if we moved camp here."

Alvin swings his tire-iron over his shoulder and says,

"I'll get on it," and turns back toward the truck.

"Those rats were sporting some interesting equipment. I don't think we've seen the last of them." The sniper muses.

Beneath all that apparatus and saltine air, she'd be attractive. "Shall we get started on the appraisal?" I inquire, as already my mind whirs with approximations, weight ratios and conversions. This isn't going to be easy but I fancy a challenge.

Callaghan straights up. "I've got to piss." She hands off her Luftgung-242, pulse rifle to Ulrich and nabs the Styllus from his holster, before walking off behind a crushed wing of the ship.

"What do you need that for?" Ulrich asks jokingly.

She screams back, "In case any of you pricks try to follow me."

We enter through the aft portion of the ship through a break in the hull. My ALC's flashlight, as well as my two employers' pair of glowrods, cast the ship in a yellowish-effulgence. The place is in shambles: torn ventilation ducts, cabling, cracks running up and down the lengths of the walls and ceilings, fallen bulkheads, ravaged storage compartments and thermal scaring. I allow Ulrich to get in front of me so that he may lead the way through the abandoned corridors.

I store the hallway's dimensions, estimated hull thickness, heat-shield, with ten to fifteen percent accountability for cabling and circuitry. The more my armlet bleeps in response to the figures, the more I realize that this is by far the greatest discovery of our century. Not even Tulloch's raising of the Titanic can account for the amount of salvageable metal that this ship will afford.

The passageways are cramped as we attempt to squeeze past fallen girders and cabling. Everything, save our footfalls against the texture-steel keeps to a disheartening silence until Ulrich breaks in, "So what do you think, Mr. Appraiser? Are we rich?" He asks while entering a new chamber.

"It's hard to tell. It all depends on what bracket you fall in – tax wise. But yea, you definitely have something here. It may take me a few days to assess everything. With something this large I have to be thorough. How did you folks find this?"

Callaghan takes up the slack. "We send out scouts on a regular basis. We just got lucky - pretty damn lucky." It's a quick answer, as if she'd been waiting for me to ask it. I pay it no mind, since it isn't my job to care.

We pass a demolished terminal designed much like those featured in the older science fiction movies: antiquated, plastic and extremely outdated. If I had a connection to the Line, I could find out just how old. I try a signal just to be sure but all I get is the familiar shifting of static and distorted imagery. Connectivity is just too weak. I add a few additional figures and then proceed into the next room.

The ship is comprised of shallow hallways that are connected to a network of secondary corridors, vaults, floor-hatches, and free-floating shafts that were used before artificial gravity was invented. Most however are intact and easily traversable, despite the decrepit state of things. There are a few areas that have collapsed entirely or will need to be scaled. I'm already making notes of these areas and what exactly we would need in order to gain access.

"How old do you think this ship is? Sixty? Seventy-years?" I asked while finishing up on some approximations.

Callaghan just brushes a strand of hair that comes too close to her eyes. "I don't know and I don't care. The sooner this is finished, the sooner we can get back to work." She pulls out another cigarette and lights it with a lazer-lighter. "Two days you said?" Smoke jets from her nostrils.

"Approximately, depends upon the weather and how many hours I'd be able to devote to my calculations. There's still a lot to cover."

"Well Mr. Burbanks," Ulrich contemplates aloud. "It

sure looks like you have your work cut out for you. How much do you think we're looking at here?"

They always ask that. "I'm guessing roughly around a thousand tons?" I always hate giving a pre-estimate because sometimes I've been known to be wrong. I'm about to reinforce my disclaimer but then we find a plaque above one of the bulk heads that makes me choke:

Christened Narthex
Terminus Alpha Centauri A
2179 CE

By the Lady herself, it's the Narthex. "It's one of ours." I whisper in a half-fear.

"My God..." Ulrich utters from his slack-jawed expression. And Callaghan's skin sinks to a greater portion of yellow.

We stand in awe for many moments, allowing the words to sink into our minds like the circling of a drain – the lost carrack has finally returned home.

"The fucking Narthex!?" Screams the petite, though large breasted, mechanic who just shortly was introduced to me as Mandy Khadolen. "You're joking right? Tell me, Luce, that you're joking."

Taking a break from her cigarettes to answer questions, Luce Callaghan keeps to an emotionless façade. "That's what the plaque said. You're acting as if we've stumbled across Pioneer or something. Junk is junk, no matter how you reason it." Beneath that cold face of ambiguity I could tell it was bothering her. It's bothering everyone.

"And metal is metal." I chime while still going over the figures to make the situation easier to digest.

"The appraiser's got a point Mandy," Ulrich says over a mug of black coffee. "You're thinking of its historical significance but it all comes down to its tonnage. That's a lot of metal out there and there aren't many private collectors interested in space relics."

"Can't we at least call someone to document it, take pictures or something before they carve it up and start shipping it out? This isn't some normal piece of machinery!"

"What do you mean?" Callaghan asks. "It looks just like every other piece of scrap we've come across, just a little bigger."

"It's the damn Narthex, Luce! It vanished during its maiden voyage to Alpha Centauri – poof – gone, just like that." The short brunet throws her arms out to portray the magical puff of smoke that engulfed it in space. "Aren't you interested? Don't you care? I mean – where is the crew? Where'd they go?"

"Since you didn't show up for your shift earlier today, I'm sure you wouldn't mind accompanying Mr. Burbank's during his tallying of the ships interior. You can let me know if you stumble across any of them."

Mandy's eyes widen. "I'm not going in there! Besides, I was working on the Mastodon's rear treads. 456 and 782 split again and I had to put on new ones. You can't make me, Luce! No way!" She crosses her arms and snubs her nose.

"Oh, I can and I will. Ulrich, ensure that Miss Khadolen makes her shift. With her share of the salvage at stake, I wouldn't want her to accidentally not show up again."

"That's not fair! I do more than my share around here—" She grabs a wrench off the table and shoves it in her belt and stomps off. "I'm never appreciated around here, I always have to do the hard jobs… can't get someone else…" Her complaints turn to mutterings as soon as she exits the tent, dropping the flap of plastivas behind her.

Ulrich laughs and hoists himself from his chair. "Well," he says in mid-stretch, "I'd better go check on the rest of the camp to see that everything is settling in all right."

He almost clears the table before Callaghan grabs his

wrist. "Keep a sharp eye about." She pauses and exchanges some unknown message with her stare. "Storm's coming."

Ulrich shifts from a grave flat-featured expression and into a half-smile. "Don't worry about a thing. I'll handle it." She releases his wrist and he continues along his way as if he hadn't been impeded. Something in her voice makes me think she wasn't talking about the weather.

Luce sits there in contemplation, lights another cigarette and lets it burn as the smoke rolls across her face. As many of those she has been sucking down today, she must have been suffering an awful withdrawal in the sniper's nest.

"Those things will kill you one day." I say as a means of striking up a conversation.

She takes another drag just to spite me. "There are worst things to die of. Besides, statistically I am more likely to die of asphyxiation from the ash, chemical poisoning or the decay. Take your pick Harmon, how do you want to die?"

"From old age if possible, 4.3 light years from here." I respond wearily as I manage to complete the last of the estimations and download the information to a dataplate. "Here's a list of my current estimates." I drop them in front of her. "They'll fluxuate as I sweep through the ship with greater detail. I'm still uncertain about a couple of the collapsed chambers and with Mandy's help I'm sure I'll be able to squeeze through with only a five-percent margin of error in estimations. It doesn't get any better than that considering the circumstances. The only thing I'm worried about is scaling the free-floating shaft in the central region of the ship, the ladder is missing or has been destroyed in the crash. I wouldn't bet much on those handholds, one slip and it's a long way down."

She does what every foreman does – looks at the figures as if they mean something and nod in agreement with the sums. It's the bottom number that they're always interested in and never like to see it go down.

Leaning back in her chair Luce asks, "Two days you

said?"

"Maybe less."

"Plan on less." She tosses the plate back to me. "And make sure Mandy goes with you."

"Don't trust me?" I ask blatantly.

"Oddly enough, I do. Theft is the least of my worries." Her eyes meet the ceiling and she fixates on the wrinkles on the tent's plastic layering, signaling that the conversation is over.

Something bothers me, be it her lack of interest in the overall figures or her emphasis on a time table. Any other foreman would be overjoyed in the discovery and the break from work, but apparently not Luce Callaghan.

I redefine my earlier dimensions of the bulkheads and scan the dark chambers with my ALC, uncovering a wide range of different metals and materials: copper, nickel, aluminum, titanium, steel and so on. The yellow-illuminated Mandy bounces excitedly behind me. I'd be lying if I said I didn't enjoy her company. Though she wears a baggy jumpsuit, there is something alluring about her that makes me constantly question whether she's naked beneath it. She is pretty. Her hair is short and brown and has Shirley Temple cheeks. I'd average that she is 4 foot 11, or 5; 89 pounds of sugar laden energy.

"Isn't this exciting?" The mechanic squeaks above the rigorous processing of my arm-terminal. "We are actually inside the Narthex. I mean, the Narthex! Aren't you excited?"

This was a completely different Khadolen than the frightened creature from the tent. "It is an unusual find but no, I'm not that excited. Chances are we'll be a miner mention in the historical archives. It's a shame we'll have to scrap it." The whole place makes me nervous. I look up a moment. "So why the sudden change? Before, you didn't even want to set foot in this place."

"Oh that? I was just pushing Luce's buttons. I knew

she was sore with me leaving her up there all day, so it was my way of turning punishment into a reward. I've wanted to get inside this thing since we first found it. You can't call yourself a mechanic if you're afraid of a ship like this. It's like the pyramids of Mars and I'm Macario Nikolayevich – ruin explorer." She cracks a child-like grin.

I finish up the analysis and move on to the next chamber with her in tow. She holds her glowrod as high as she can whilst examining the antiquated marvel.

"I can't imagine the work and love that has been put into this ship. This was the first of the initial carracks sent out after the cataclysm. The fifty-population crew was put into hibernation chambers and whoosh! off they went into the loneliness of space."

"So what happened?"

"No one knows. Just vanished! Communication was lost and people started believing in space monsters." She claws her fingers just to emphasize her point. "Took em' ten years before people were brave enough to try it again." She sniffs the air with a like-familiarity. "Do you smell that?"

"Smell what?" I ask astounded by the absolute randomness of the question.

"It smells like..." She sniffs again and hesitates. "I don't know... like sex in here."

We emerge in, what looks to be, the storage bay – a twenty-foot high massive room filled with unmarked alumiplast crates, some the size of a pet carrier, whilst others larger than a transport vehicle. Personally, I didn't smell a thing. The stillness about the place is enough to put me on edge.

The bay extends deeply into the bowels of the ship and the luminance off the glowrod only extends thirty feet before it's lost amidst the darkness. I'm about to comment on phantom senses, caused by taking one too many lunar sticks, before I hear something sliding across the textured flooring.

I pull the 38 from my pocket, still resting there from

earlier today. Mandy is silent for a moment and quietly replaces the glowrod with a wrench sitting inside her tool belt.

"Tools of the trade?" She whispers while holding the wrench up to her face and then follows with an uncertain, "I thought projectile weapons are illegal."

I try and hush her without giving myself away. "Ulrich gave it to me." As if that was enough in justification.

The noise sounded like it came from further inside the storage bay, perhaps craftily hidden among the maze of damaged equipment and crates. Mandy grabs my free hand and shuffles up close to me. I can smell the strength of her perfume, Annulla Roberts mixed with engine lubricant. She smiles when she presses her body up against mine, a means of securing my whereabouts and whispers, "Hope you like girls."

It may have been possible for one of the junk-rats to have snuck inside the ship, has lined his pockets and is waiting for the opportune moment to escape. Perhaps an animal, a pet of some kind, has wandered inside and became lost. But when I mention the possibility to Mandy she just shakes her head and tells me that they don't have any.

We curb around a few piles of boxes, shining the light into the shadows in order to dissuade our growing anxieties. The both of us strive to keep our footfalls light, but one can only do so much with rubber soles and metal. As I stop to listen, Mandy squeezes my hand in believing that I had heard something. I give her reassurance as I press forward and after rounding the next aisles of cargo, our lights shine across a pale figure sprawled across the ground without any clothes or articles to cover it. The two of us gasp in astonishment at the naked woman.

"Go get Ulrich and Callaghan." I tell her. When she doesn't respond I yell, "Now!" And without any further moment of hesitation the tiny mechanic sprints off, taking the light with her.

I throw my ALC into hibernation mode and turn on the

built-in flashlight. I kneel down over her form, shinning the light across her body, which refracts in a smooth plastic-like reflection; igniting her skin in a brilliant halo. Afraid to touch her, I shift around her counter clockwise, trying to discover whether she's alive or not. Despite her vulnerability, I keep the pistol trained on her just in case. I stare at her for minutes, and for all sense of purpose believe her to be dead, until I notice a minuscule raise in her chest, unnoticeable from a distance, but slight enough to indicate life.

I'd like nothing more than to check her pulse, pick her up and take her to whatever ramshackle medical facilities are aboard the Mastodon, but reason warns me not to. The way her skin responds to the light isn't natural. It's possible that she could be infected.

As I lean in, she stirs! kicking a close cargo container in response to a spasm and I fall backwards in terror. As I strike the ground, I pull the trigger but the weapon remains silent. A good thing, as I probably would have killed her. The safety is on. Once I am able to get a hold of myself, I put the gun back in my pocket so there won't be any future accidents.

I caress the beam over her face. Her features couldn't have been chiseled finer on marble. Her hair is thin, though plentifully white like spun platinum threads, with a metallic sheen to it. I can't help myself from reaching out and touching it, to prove to myself that it is indeed human hair. It feels like synthesized spider silk as I rub it through my fingers. A strange aroma filters past my nose and it tickles, and for a moment smells foul, until something shifts, and I catch wind of the very scent that Mandy had mentioned which is near overwhelming. I lift a tuft of her hair up to my face for a closer whiff, but before I have a chance to inhale, my wrist is seized by the woman's frigid hand!

My heart turns cold, she draws me to her face and I meet her ignited emerald eyes when she whispers, "…storm's coming."

The woman fainted immediately after she spoke but she left me with a lingering sense of dread and to my surprise, a bruised imprint of her hand across my skin. I am commissioned by Ulrich and Callaghan, due to my involuntary contact with her, to carry her freezing body into one of the rooms of the medical ward inside the Mastodon and forced to remain for examination.

I'm introduced to Dr. Seiger Reins, a dark haired man whose eyes are glazed over from blindness with the standard optical implants that bubble out from his temples. The red lights of his lenses scan over me with particular interest in my injury.

"You don't happen to have hemophilia in your family, do you Mr. Burbanks?"

Ulrich snickers from beneath the ward's threshold, where both he and the straight-faced Luce lean in patience. "Maybe he's just sensitive Doc, he's from the city after all."

Seiger keeps an apathetic charm. "Did it hurt when she grabbed you?"

I shake my head. "Just startled me."

"Does it hurt now?"

"It's a bit sore." I admit.

He sighs from some secret frustration. "Nothing's broken." He tosses me a roll of gauze. "Wrap it. Tell me if it gets worse."

He's not very reassuring or comforting but then again the man is blind. I hear they don't give any anesthetic while connecting nerves to those things. Something to do with ensuring the synapses aren't muddled. The pain he suffered must have been indescribable. It must be difficult to hold sympathies for others after experiencing something like that. But like everyone else in the room he's more interested in the mysterious girl than a minor wrist bruise.

"What's wrong with her skin?" I ask while peeling off the first roll of tape.

"She's not sick, if that's what you mean." He runs his

hand over her arm and pinches her skin together to read some unknown reaction. He then holds her at the brow and examines the discoloration of her eyelids and surrounding tissue that appear as a multitude of black and purples. "I'd say albino, but it doesn't explain the reason her skin reacts so peculiar to light. I will need to do some blood work, take some skin samples, but all in all, I'd need access to the Line in order to make comparisons. I have contacts with the Lycian Corporation who specialize in environment mutations. Who knows what kind of things that ship has been exposed to?"

"If she's not sick, then what's wrong with her?" Luce asks soberly.

The doctor pays her no mind. "Beyond the obvious?" He checks her pulse. "She's suffering from PHS, prolonged hibernation syndrome. This specimen has just recently crawled out of a bed without any counteractive agent, so she's waking up the hard way." He turns to the pair in the doorway. "I suggest leaving her here for observation and I'll let you know as soon as she's able to speak."

The foreman presses with absolute disregard. "How long will that be?"

Dr. Reins stands firm. "Not for awhile. She's lucky to have been able to make use of her limbs. Her temperature is at a constant 68 degrees, her eyes are dilated, and the venom pumped into her veins takes awhile – without proper chemicals – to break down. It could be any where from a couple days to a couple weeks."

"So, she'll recover?" Luce's eyes narrow and a shred of darkness that she'd been holing up inside herself creeps out.

The doctor merely blinks in a programmed response. "Yes – in time, I suppose she will."

"That's it then!" Luce exhales in a harsh fashion and slams her open palms against the wall. "It's all over! Ulrich, tell the men to pack their shit, we're getting the hell out of here."

He somberly straightens. "Yes, ma'am."

"Wait a minute!" I jump off the examination table and hastily try and halt her escape. "You're leaving? The Narthex. The ship..." I gather my words. "You're leaving the ship?!"

Callaghan's eyes bear into me like a volley of poisonous quills. "The claim is gone! Despite all the work that was done in order to acquire it. If she's coming out of hibernation, it means she's a crew member, which means that she is the sole living inheritor of the ship and all its property." She grinds her teeth. "Am I right?"

Her voice, her tone; I cannot say, but I am afraid of her. I dare not answer her – she's right. We all know she's right. The crimson haired woman only scowls at my lack in response and walks off in huff, throwing violent echoes throughout the Mastodon from whatever object she encounters.

Once she's a fair distance away, Ulrich shrugs his shoulders. "Tough luck, Harmon – just when things were going so well. One thing you learn about Lucile is that she's quick to temper; give her some time to cool off and she comes to her senses."

"But the ship? We're not leaving are we?" I ask out of desperation.

"Are you kidding? After everything we've gone through. I wouldn't leave if my life depended on it." Ulrick rubs his chin in forethought. "Rescuing the former crew of the Narthex has to amount to something." He smiles slightly and places his hands on my shoulders for reassurance. "Not like your job is affected. Take the rest of the day off, tomorrow I'll need you to continue your appraisal. Must be nice not having a stake in the claim." He slips away and steps over the six-inch frame before looking back over his shoulder. "We're counting on you, Harmon."

"What about the rest of the Narthex crew?" I quickly ask.

"Don't worry. I'll take care of it." His voice is distant,

as if he is thinking of something unrelated at the time of his answer. I don't have time to question him about it, as he disappears round the corner.

"It's interesting how much one individual matters, isn't it Mr. Burbanks." I spin around and catch the doctor loading a concoction into a 3½ pound stainless steel injection-gun. "Assist me for a moment." He motions to the woman's legs.

"What's that?" I inquire while nodding toward the shiny instrument.

"Something to get her body temperature up. She won't like it. Hold her down – legs, if you please." He draws back the lever of the device and a small hiss emits from its inner chambers.

"You think she'll live then?" I grab hold of her ankles while Seiger puts a biting stick inside her mouth.

"She'll recover, yes. What happens outside my ward is something else." He taps at a place in her neck to bring up the vein.

"What exactly do you mean by that?"

His red eye lights glow from across me. "Ready... 2...1..." He injects her with the serum and slams the tool on the side of the table while quickly throwing himself on her upper torso, pinning her arms to the plastic table. The woman is forced to heavy breathing, as her body starts to spasm, her legs kick, her toes and fingers curl and the stick groans under the pressure of her jaw. It's over in a few blinks and she falls back to a motionless slumber.

"Outside this ward," he continues from earlier, as he releases his grip and takes a deep breath, "is a dangerous place. Plenty of things can go wrong."

"Like the decay?" I retort, unsure of what he is getting at.

Dr. Reins smoothes his hair back from the turmoil. "Yes..." He picks up his injection tool and walks to a side terminal, "...like the decay." There is a touch of regret in his voice. "Now if you don't mind Mr. Burbanks, I have a lot of work to do."

I go to leave but before I make it over the step the doctor reminds me, "Be sure to visit me if that wrist gets any worse; any change at all, you understand?" His voice is monotone but filled with the concern of his occupation.

I nod before leaving the room.

I wander for hours looking for something to do. My ALC stilled buzzes with the interference of the overcast. Had it not been for those clouds I would be able to reach the pylons. Were it not for those clouds there'd be a whole lot of other things. What I would give to be able to booster the reception and continue through my playlist, possibly even catch up on the news. I believe that more than anything I just want something to occupy my mind with, to be able to relieve my anxieties of all that has happened. I think wishing is getting the better of me.

My thoughts are usurped after exiting the Mastodon, when I see the orange suited Khadolen standing at just the edge of the camp, staring at the obelisk-like structure of the Narthex. The laborers bustle about the bivouac, keeping in conversation about their newly acquired gains, Luce must not have told them yet. All seem to ignore the petite mechanic. Her brown hair flutters lightly in a virgin breeze. After a brief stroll through the camp, I end at her side. Her eyelashes twitch from the intrusion of her peripheral but doesn't say a word, preferring to stare out across the ship, pondering things that I can't imagine.

I look out, catching the same wind that is holding her in place. A peculiar feeling starts to grow, an anxiety of sorts that builds the more my mind spirals about the crashed carrack, twisting about the blackness of its outer hull and wrapping itself around questions I don't know how to ask. We bask at the edge of fear and discovery, together locked in a quizzical thought – the notion that something terrible may come, like some prophetic omen.

Mandy keeps silent for some time, refusing to say a word. She just stands there, failing to acknowledge my arrival or give any sign that may designate her part of the waking world. It is only after a few minutes which pass with every emphasis on the second that she acquires the courage to break free from her fixation, slightly whispering to the ash, "There's something…terribly wrong, do you see? No…? Something…" without making any motion as to point out what it is that she's referring to.

I look, tracing my eyes down the lengths of its exposed beams, scarred hull and cracked exterior. I take in the charred shape like it's some geometric miracle and then cast my vision about it like a pebble down a chasm. I see nothing that has laid cause for its transformation from the curious to the uncanny. Just the same, it's there.

"No, I…" but no sooner do those words escape my lips that a tightness squeezes in my chest, my hands start trembling and my forehead starts to perspire, "Yes…" I see shadows where there shouldn't be shadows, dark recesses where hidden things are kept, and the haunting feeling that something unknown lurks amidst its empty corridors. I swallow hard as the thoughts play into me, like a ghost story told around a campfire. The Narthex has taken up a persona that I hadn't noticed till now, a slight change in existence, enough to put my hairs on end and make me question my perceptions. It frightens me, but I dare not pinpoint why.

Mandy takes up my hand, pondering the impossible thought. "There's something eerie about it." She pauses, "I don't know what it is. Or maybe…"

I nod in agreement, keeping my eyes poised on the spacecraft, looking for that very thing that has triggered this uneasiness.

"You know that feeling you get, when you lay awake at night, thinking about the void that comes after death?" She takes a quick breath and at the same time a foreign wind presses through the cracks of the ship, giving way to a slight howl. "When I look at that ship, it reminds me of death – the ultimate end; the dark, empty, quiet of space. I wonder if the crew dreamed while they were in hibernation, and when they ran out of things to dream, if they slipped into the near-nothingness of death? How long were they there? I just can't imagine it, Harmon. I just can't imagine it."

Mandy's eyes soak with the burden of her reverie. I comfort her as best as I can, hugging her close but never looking away from the colossal artifact. She feels for the crease of my back and I roll my arm over her shoulder. I expect to be overwhelmed with her personal scent and perfume, but my nostrils are struck with a tinge of melted rust and sulphur. The both of us sniff the air, attempting to trace its source and shortly thereafter I get the taste of copper in my mouth.

"Shit!" She squirms away from me. "Shit! Shit! Shit!" She repeats over and over again as she scrambles back toward the encampment.

"Why? What's wrong?"

She halts momentarily enough to say, "Move your ass Harmon! Ash is coming, and coming fast!"

The ship takes to wailing and tiny ash-devils fly up from the desert floor. I throw up my ventilator quickly in remembering what Alvin had said – "a face full of ash." The winds grow from out of the horizon, scraping across the desert floor like an army of invisible claws. It isn't but a millisecond that I'm hit square in the face by a cloud of ash; blinding me in its fury. A crack of thunder strikes overhead and I almost lose my footing. Mandy returns to help me, grabbing around my waist and steering me in the direction of the crawler; my eyes burning. As we frantically rush for cover, I can see the blurred silhouettes of the dirt-movers struggling to bring left-out equipment into the Mastodon's back end, and tearing down canopies to cover important pieces of machinery beneath the blaring of the warning sirens.

The two of us rush up a side ramp and when we've

cleared the overhang, Mandy pushes me to my knees and pulls a water bottle from out of a wall cabinet. She shoves her fingers into my eyes, peels them open and jets liquid into them. The pain is short but immense!

She grabs me by the cheeks to align with her face. "Can you see all right?! Harmon, can you see me?"

I nod my head frantically so that I may break from her grasp to rub my swollen eyes.

"Good boy!" She kisses me quickly on the lips and rushes back down the ramp shouting back at me, "Stay there!" She dons a ventilator and slaps on a pair of goggles. She does it so quickly like habit.

I see her tiny figure joining the rest of the road recyclers, grabbing bits of equipment as they're passed onto her, regardless of her small size. Both men and women rush through the dust and maelstrom that threatens overhead, skirting among one another to ensure that every detail is covered in preparation of the coming weather. They work in synchrony, a single unit, a single entity, poised on preserving what little material they own. I reflect on how stricken the two of us had been just moments before and how suddenly she managed to adapt, and how I just stumbled in the dark. It's at this moment that I realize what it is to live beyond the fringes, where it seems everything is against you, and how in the end all you have are the people around you. In a second everything can change.

I watch as the clouds of soot take demonic shapes, all stampeding across the plain, all heading in one direction, rampaging at the call of lightening that grows closer by the moment. In its fury, I lose track of who's who. Mandy disappears in a blast of dust and merges with the rest of the shadows of people. Thunderclaps roar overhead, as the crew finish their preparations and are rounded up by a dust covered Lucille. Together they race inside before the rain swoops in, dousing the ground in an audacious torrent. I am pushed to standing as the stench of sweat, dirt, and sulphur crowds into the foyer. The door to the outside is magnetically shut, leaving nothing but the sound of heavy breathing and the drumming of rain.

I search for Mandy to see if she made it inside but all I see are gray faces all blanketed by flakes of charcoal.

"Did everyone get in?" Luce screams over the pounding of rain. "Did anyone get burned?" No one says a word, as many are too busy pulling off their facemasks to then wipe the dirt from their brow.

A curdled scream erupts from outside. One of the laborers points out one of the windows. "It's Hendrix! The stupid bastard is still out there!" All push to get their view. A wide-eyed plague sweeps through the vestibule, pale complexions, as they watch in stark horror as a fellow worker fights against the rains, his arms flailing about, trying to shield himself from the acidic-waters, his flesh blistering in the downpour as flakes of his skin break off from the blasts of debris.

"Suit me up!" Luce roars.

Everyone rushes to side lockers that rest a few feet from the doors, they tear into them, each retrieving rubber components: boots, gloves, torso, legs, each complicated by rows of straps and buckles. They do exactly as she orders, with her hopping inside the boots while the rest of them throw the layers of rubber body armor across her figure and tighten it to ensure little chance of a leak.

"Base canisters! Have them ready!"

A few men break off from their workings and rip open a few aluminum doors marked with a red cross, stealing large tanks fitted with a hose and nozzle.

When everything is set, I am pulled out of the vestibule and into a side compartment with the rest of the crew, where the doors shut, sealing Callaghan within. The portal to the outside opens and a flood of rain sizzles into the room. She batters against the tough winds, down the ramp and toward the exposed and now collapsed Hendrix; the sound of acid pattering against her suit. The rest of us stare from the Mastodon's portholes, as she gathers her fallen comrade and hoists him with all her power onto her shoulder.

A barrage of wind lays siege against her as she rushes up the ramp, fighting to keep her balance. Once the door shuts behind her and we hear that familiar hissing of the locks, do the men pour into the adjacent room, to release the chalky powder in streams out their canisters across their two smoking forms. I am struck by the timed order of things, the precision in which everyone does their part. After the powder settles, the rain now turned to clumps of grit, do the laborers hoist the black and red Hendrix off Lucille's shoulder and rush him quickly down the hallway towards the medical ward.

She pulls the rubber mask off her face, breathing hard into the floor, her knees caught beneath her as she rests from the ordeal. A few workers stay behind and offer her a helping hand, but she slaps them away; preferring to get up on her own. She tosses off the gloves then scratches profusely at the rest of the buckles that imprison her. She kicks off the boots and struggles beneath the awkwardness of the suit.

"Get out! All of you get out!" She throws a boot against the wall, the deep bang only serving to emphasize her point.

And when they all disappear into the rooms beyond, the men too afraid to stay, I stand by, just around the corner, to keep myself hidden and available if needed. My heart breaks as when everyone is gone, that Lucille throws herself against one of the lockers, pulls her head into her hands, slides down into a huddled position and cries.

I learn that Mandy made it in through the rear of the Mastodon just before the rain hit. I'd give anything to be with her right now, but as things are she's got more work to do. The storm just happened to complicate things for her, a leak somewhere in the higher floors. Now it's just Luce and I, sitting nearby as Seiger returns from his visitation with Hendrix.

"I'm afraid there isn't anything I can do. If it was just the acid burns he'd be able to live but he breathed in too much ash. The force of the wind was enough to strip him of his epidermis. I'm barely keeping him alive." His lenses scan over us both of us for some response but I think I am too numb to it all. "I found this." He hands Callaghan a brick-size piece of metal. "I had to cut it from his fingers. I'm guessing you know where it came from."

Callaghan turns it over in her hands, studying it as if the whole thing was foreign to her but then her face grows cold and distant. "He was new. Thought he'd help himself." She snickers sorrowfully. "He made me laugh. That's why I hired him on. He was a good man. He has a family I think. Saw and opportunity and he took it." She hands me the brick. "How much, Harmon?"

I weight the thing in my hand; 12 lbs. I don't bother scanning it for impurities, trace metals or hidden compositions, no need to be accurate. "1042.8 credits, a couple months mortgage... approximately." I try to hand it back to her but she refuses to even look at it.

"The fool! The God damn fool! He must have felt reason to –" Her face flattens, her eyes narrow and her cheeks sink beneath the weight of her thoughts. She looks over toward the unconscious woman who still rests in shallow breath atop one of the examination tables. Lucile doesn't say a word.

She stares for what seems to be an eternity as Seiger lays out Hendrix's condition, "I give him a little less than an hour. I gave him something for the pain. He should pass without discomfort." He turns to me and says. "An unfortunate trend, I'm afraid." The doctor leaves and returns to his patient's side ensuring that he isn't alone in his final moments – compassionate after all.

The foreman's eyes are wet with her thoughts, thoughts

that causes her face to tense and writhe with malice. I dare not say anything to her, but I know that I shouldn't leave this place; that I should remain. And in that, she turns her eyes on me, just briefly, before standing from her chair and walking out of the room announcing. "I've a letter to write."

Later in the night, after the rains have slowed and their fearsome echoes have dwindled to a light sprinkle, I am left alone with the mysterious woman in the dimness of the medical ward. It is upon Dr. Reins request that I watch over her a shift. I turn the brick in my hands, discovering the different materials and contemplate its overall design – it looks like it was cut with a wielding torch. I glance occasionally at her form stretched delicately beneath the warmth of the thermal sheet. She is whiter than the linen, and the dark pigmentation around her eyes creates the illusion of empty sockets. A few florescent lights illuminate the ward, bathing the woman's skin in a purifying glow, while reflecting wisps of incandescence that dance on the wall.

I watch her, contemplating the hidden secrets that lie within the Narthex, the places it has seen and the events that kidnapped it from its destination. I meditate on what Mandy had said, about the fear of the abyss that waits for us all. I lean my head back in thought.

I drift, for what it seems, down a river; the sensation of floating playing out across my body. I can see the emerald meadows of Alpha Centauri, the winds brushing against the tandiss leaves and hera blooms. Somewhere I hear the sound of children laughing, as they play among the tall grasses and dance to the songs of the epick birds. I hear a woman's ethereal voice singing from beneath a hill. She's draped in a pearly silk, her hair tied in ribbons, with a large wicker basket resting off her hip.

We are brought together in this dream, looking into each others eyes; hers filled with a brilliant blue. Her skin catches the splendor of the white glow of the sun. We are soothed by the warm breezes of a mid-summer afternoon. Her lips are wet in anticipation, as she brings her hands up to touch my face.

When I open my eyes I find myself back in the cold company of the Mastodon, the pallid-woman, now sitting atop my lap, caressing my cheeks.

"Seima." Comes her whisper. My head swims with euphoria as she presses her naked body against me, rubbing her cold skin against my own. She fondles my sides, "You know that feeling you get," she kisses my neck. "When you lay awake at night..." Her lips are like ice that burns into my skin and flows through the rest of me like some nefarious poison.

My mind snaps to reality, shrugging off whatever spell she had cast on me. I struggle to push her off but she grabs my wrist, and I scream! but the sound yields to the assault of the heavy rains above, as her grip burns at my flesh; smoke rising from the wound like acid. Her eyes are as black as coals.

"Do you think about the void that comes after death?" A pair of brilliantly glowing wings unfolds from her back, which scintillate from the overhead bulbs. She rears her head with an intake of breath, revealing a row of jagged shark's teeth.

I can hear the groaning of the ceiling above me, the twisting of metal, bending against some immeasurable weight. She grabs my face and jerks it to her own. "Can you see me?"

The roof collapses, throwing a waterfall of rain overtop the two of us. My heart screams, as she kisses me deeply as a lover would, while our skin blisters beneath the chemicals, her wings enveloping us both. "Good boy..." echoes her voice as I throttle myself awake.

The woman sleeps across the way, the ceiling intact; everything as it was. I wipe my face to extinguish the jitters that have crept into my hands and the images out of my head.

I curb my position on the chair and watch as the wisps dance methodically against the steel walls of the medical ward.

After being relieved by Alvin, I spend the rest of the night in a room that has been set aside for me, away from the typically crew's quarters, to forget the nightmarish dream.

Nourishment has been left for me on my bed, a few portions of reprocessed food tucked inside silver packets, along with a bottle of water. I suppose a formal sit down meal was too much to expect; rustic, very rustic.

It is not long before I tear off the tops of them with my teeth that I hear the opening of my door and see a tiny figure slipping in through the gap with a clear bottle in her hand.

"Oh!" She turns and raps on the metallic frame and bites her lower lip. "I'm sorry I didn't come back right away. I had a lot of work to do. Just when you think it's all done, something breaks, and off I go." She thrusts the bottle forward and makes it dance from side to side. "Want a drink?"

She's wearing a white tank top and a short pair of skin tight shorts. I wave her to come in, her face brightening up at the gesture. She closes the door behind her and then bounces on the spot next to me on the bed. She hands me the bottle. It's a chardonnay. I don't recognize its label. I needed a drinking partner. Sorry, I don't have any glasses."

"What are we drinking to?" I ask.

"Another day of life." She flashes a half-cocked smile and smoothes out the invisible hairs on her arms.

"I'm sorry about your crewmate." I say while I struggle to get the cap off. How I miss the old cork bottles.

Mandy's smile disappears into a far distant look. "Yea - tough luck, right? Thought he could make it without wearing a mask. Probably was already in the process of nabbing a portion of the metal when the storm caught him off guard – maybe he was inside the Narthex the entire time and was waiting to make it out before anyone saw. I don't know.

None of us foresaw it coming." She grabs the bottle from me, makes a few snaps against the plastic cap and pops it off within a blink; taking a swig off the top before passing it to me. "He was new. I don't like to talk about when things like this happen. I just want to forget and look forward." Her countenance lightens from beneath the drudgery of the conversation. "What do you look forward to, Harmon?"

"Well, for starters." I delve into the etiquette of the moment, tasting a good portion of the chardonnay. "I'd like to get back to the pylons so I can have access to the Line again. I usually listen to music before I go to sleep."

She pokes me in the ribs when I'm about to take another drink, almost causing me to spill. "No, I mean long-term! What do you look forward to?" She asks while giggling at my near accident with the wine.

"I want to fly my own ship and see what all is out there, maybe catch up with everyone else at Alpha Centauri; explore the galaxy. That sort of thing. But that may never happen." I chuckle when one does at something typical. "I can't even afford a ground vehicle."

Mandy takes the bottle from me, the scent of alcohol finally breathing into the room. "I've always wanted to work on one of the barges that sail out of here once a year. Just being able to feel the vibrations of the engines beneath my feet and my hands being that which keeps everything afloat is what I always dreamed of. You have to be good. To give her all you got. I figure if I can make it all the way to Alpha Centauri, that I would have my fill." She falls backward and lands backside on the mattress.

"So why are you out here?" I ask.

"References, experience. I figure that if I could make it out past the fringes, then I would be able to handle anything. Besides, it's good money. I think that's why everyone else does it – for the money; then, there is the occasional salvage. Looks like we're screwed on this one, huh?"

"Seems that way." I stare blankly ahead, thinking

about Hendrix and everything he meant to sacrifice just to get his hands on a piece of the ship. Perhaps he was one of the few who noticed us lifting the girl from the Narthex and knew that by law it was no longer theirs. I couldn't get his screams out of my head or how the storm nearly –

"Hey, Mister?" Mandy sets the bottle aside and looks me in the eyes; a tigress on her back. "Are you going to sit there or are you going to kiss me?"

Images of Hendrix vanishes in her eyes, as I lean down, wrapping my arms around her torso, pressing my lips against hers and giving into the smell of Annulla Roberts and engine oil. In her embrace, how easily I forget all that has transpired.

We're wakened by a banging against the steel door of my room, with Ulrich's voice bellowing through the cracks. "Harmon! Get the hell up! We've got trouble!"

I hit the switch nearest the bed and the florescent lights crackle to life. Mandy and I give each other a concerned, though confused, glance before jetting out of bed and into our clothes. "Be right there!" I yell. "One thing after another, huh?" I ask while Mandy slips into her top.

She's already lifting the latch to the door before I'm able to secure my ALC to my wrist. I pocket the 38 just in case before stepping out into the hallway.

Ulrich hasn't had time to shave, a few bristles decorate his face and his hair is all matted – he mustn't have had time to shower either. He does a double take and raises an eyebrow. "Well, hello, Mandy." He chuckles lightly, but I can tell by how his Styllus is free from its holster that it wasn't the time for tomfoolery.

"What's going on?" I ask sleepy-eyed.

"I'll tell you on the way, follow me." And he rushes off down the hallway.

I do my best to keep stride with Mandy in tow. I can tell by her breathing that she wouldn't mind having longer legs.

"A couple men from the crew attempted to kill that woman we found. Alvin tried to intervene but there were five of them. Alvin's a big guy, but he can only do so much. He was knocked unconscious for a short while but when he came to he found two of them with their throats ripped out and the woman gone."

"Who was it?" Mandy chokes out.

"Jenson, Van Doren, Reynolds, Kaphrey, and Ferrell; Kaphrey and Ferrell were the ones who got it."

"Their throats were ripped out? How?" I asked perplexed.

"Seiger thinks she used her hands. That little girl is full of surprises, may be a bit stronger than what we thought. That's only a fraction of the problem! Word's out and now everyone's in a panic. A couple people broke into the weapons locker and they are now choosing sides – it's a bloody fox hunt! Worst yet, I can't find Callaghan anywhere! If we can find her then we can end this. It's not like her to disappear like this."

"I don't follow."

"Luce frightens people. You get her at the end of that rifle of hers and it's all over; she doesn't give a damn who you are, she'll take your head clean off at any range. Hell, she even scares me at times." We stop at one of the few elevators that descend to the lower-levels of the Mastodon. "You two head to the ground floor, see if you can find either Lucile or that woman. The crew has seen you around so they won't bother you unless you give them a reason. You'll both be fine."

"But what happens if she objects to being found?"

"Then shoot her! It'll be better off for everyone that way."

"What happens once we find them?" Mandy demands.

"If it's Luce, find me, if it's that woman, then hide her or get the fuck out of here." With that, Ulrich tightens his grip on his Styllus and runs the rest of the corridor.

Taking the elevator, the two of us reach the bottom level. The Mastodon is quiet, a quiescence that reminds me of the Narthex and its inactivity, which only adds to my apprehensions. Mandy keeps pressed against me as we search through the vacant corridors and empty rooms. The colossal-crawler was built for efficiency, and so there many nooks and crannies for one to hide in, as cabling, storage compartments, and ducts extend down into the living space, making it difficult to find those things not wishing to be found.

"There have been days where I go about my work..." Mandy whispers after a long moment of silence, "...and never see a soul." She grabs my hand to ensure we won't be separated.

"How many people live in this thing?" I ask while turning down a neighboring corridor.

"Around thirty or so. Both men and women. People keep to themselves; small social circles and the like. At night, people get drunk. You can hear their laughter and love making echo through the grating; everyone living in the present, ignoring the dangers of the outside as best as they can."

"What about you?"

She beams a heart-throbbing smile. "I keep to myself. Though, I've had offers. I just hadn't found the right drinking partner, I guess." She winks at me.

We turn into the kitchen and halt a few feet shy of the frame. Inside are six men, two women, with holstered pistols, a few with rifles, knives and all manner of miscellaneous items to bludgeon someone to death. Three of the men surround the center table looking over the blueprints of the Mastodon, a few others relaxing, one eating. They all whisper between one another, making what they say barely audible – they're looking for her, plotting points and making notes.

They eye us suspiciously, caught between thoughts of action. One man, short black hair, rugged complexion, slowly straightens to make himself look bigger; while the woman by the refrigerator, somewhere in her twenties, long blonde hair, unbuttons the straps on her Wulfvenstats-141 pistol, and rests a hand on its handle; a man in the corner, sets his food down on his plate and puts a hand up on the table to give him a moments boost.

Mandy tugs at my hand. My eyes are transfixed and unwilling to leave the room. "Come on! This is not the place for us."

She nearly tips me over when she pulls, and I have to reposition my feet so as not to leave a facial imprint on the textured steel flooring. I am half-expecting a few laughs from that blunder but all that comes after is disquietude and a grim paranoia of being followed as we continue down a different section of the habitation.

"That was Jenson and Reynolds at the table." Mandy whispers once we're out of earshot. "We want to avoid them as much as possible. Tensions are high enough as they are."

I try and defend myself. "But they aren't after us."

"I know but if they knew what we were up to, I don't know what they'd do." Her teeth chatter during a deep breath in air.

I hear voices coming from around a side passage and immediately Mandy seizes my wrist and drags me into an adjoining room. She presses me up against the inner wall, trying to keep us out of sight as the voices approach. We are in storage of sorts, a few containers of food stuffs rest off to the side as well as some cleaning supplies; mops and the like. By the sounds of their footfalls there are two of them.

I take in a breath to whisper, but Mandy halts me with a finger over my lips. She shakes her head to emphasize the gesture. In moments, the two pass without notice and continue down the hallway without halting.

She removes her finger as she eases back into herself.

"Why are we hiding?" I ask in whisper.

"Harmon – there's something I have to tell you about

the people here. They're –"

Another pair of voices catches us by surprise, but rather than coming from out in the hallway it seems to be emanating from below us. Not far from our feet is a perforated access panel, sometimes used to travel more efficiently between floors. The voice is familiar. It's Lucille.

"I want that bitch found and I want her found now!" She says as her shadow falls into view.

A man's voice chirps in. "We're looking as best as we can. We've already swept the top floors, made a good search of it too, so there shouldn't be long before we find her. She's bound to be around here some where."

"Listen to me – I don't care how you find her just do it quickly. I don't know how the five of you managed to fuck things up this badly."

"She came out of no where, Luce. It was like she was expecting us."

"Just make sure that when you find her you make sure that she never wakes up again, you got it?"

Their shadows disappear farther into the room and it's not long before their voices are gone entirely. It is at this moment that I realize the severity of the situation.

"I think Luce is trying to kill that woman." I whisper to Mandy.

"That's what I was going to tell you, Harmon. The majority of people here are ex-military. Luce herself served in the Christian Wars. It's not that I have anything against the military, it's just that I've heard things – rumors and such – and none of them good."

"What sort of things?" I wonder as my heart starts to pain me with threats of anxiety.

"The type of things you don't want to repeat." She grabs my hand. "Come on, we have to find her before the rest of them do."

We stumble into the rear storage of the Mastodon where the trucks and equipment, saved from last night, are stored. The bay consists of a 20 foot ceiling, supported by thick beams of steel and iron girders. The 50 foot long vault is cluttered by alumiplast cargo containers, spare drill bits, pile drivers and stationary cranes. It seems that after everyone rushed inside with the equipment, that no one was willing to clean out the mess that blew in with the winds. The massive two story metal doors dominate the rear of the Mastodon, magnetically shut from last night's storm.

I look about hoping to catch some glimmer of movement, but nothing. "You'd think they'd have someone covering the exit." And then the smell hits me.

My side companion pulls me down to ear-level and whispers, "I think she's here." Her nose twitching to the malodor.

I swallow a lump that had just hardened inside my throat and I bring my hand up to my chest to speed its progression. My hands sweat and Mandy's grip only tightens as we creep stealthily into the maze of cargo.

Our breaths are light and sometimes I wonder whether Mandy is breathing at all. The place has taken to the sinister, as if the shadows are longer than they should, that the boxes shift a few inches from last I saw, or that passages between the aisles of equipment distort, appearing distant and frightening. It is as if I've fallen into some state of vertigo, such in fact that our fears rapidly multiply between each sound that spews from the above ventilation system.

Our delusions are rewarded as my heart skips a painful beat when my eyes lock onto a trail of human blood, glistening from the overhanging lamps. I keep my free hand in my pocket and squeezed on the handle of the 38. And as we round the corner of one of the larger containers, I nearly avoid putting a hole in my clothing as the rounded face of something familiar collides into us – Alvin Stencil, thank God!

"Mr. Burbanks, Miss Khaldolen, it's you!" The shaggy haired man exclaims as he struggles to catch his breath. "You scared the bejesus out of me." The tire iron he carries lowers significantly to his side. "What are you two doing here?" His head is covered in a taped bandage.

Mandy is first to answer. "Looking for that woman. What are you doing here?"

"Same, Ulrich got to me earlier and told me to poke around in the rear storage and get one of the trucks ready if things get too rough. It looks like it has done just that... I heard a noise, followed the trail and...," he swallows. "...it doesn't look pretty."

"Who is it this time?" Mandy probes for detail, her face riddled with angst.

Alvin looks off over her shoulder, as if the answer would be hiding some place else, anything to avoid eye contact. "I, I can't tell."

She bites her upper lip and manages a short sentence. "Show me."

Together they follow the line of crimson. I manage just a few feet behind, until last night's spectacle replays in my thoughts and I stop just short from the location; refusing to view any additional scenes of ghoulishness. I lean my shoulder against one of the alumiplast crates as nausea stabs into my stomach and acid threatens to work its way up my throat. I feel sick, feverous and tired. Dizziness sets in and I do all I can to steady my balance and try to focus on something. I start to wonder what it is that's come over me, as my nose is assaulted by a mixture of varying senses: of lavender, decay, and –

Good boy.

I hear it echo from behind me and I spin painfully around – in horror of what I may find - to come face to face with the waxy skinned woman, the discolored tissue around her eyes only heightening the whites of her corneas. I stand completely still, precast in whatever ghastly expression that fear can only bring, as she stares at me in an emotionless fix. Her naked form glows with the refractions of light. Her hands reach up, her red stained fingers extending between an assortment of distances, as if piercing between worlds, trailing in a ghostly blur, before finding their way to my face. Her touch is cool, a counteragent amidst my fever, as she cups her hands against my cheeks as if checking to see if I were real. Then, in one swift movement, when convinced of my end, she throws herself against me, embracing me as if I were the first person she's seen in a world filled with monsters.

After a quick breath and shiver of relief, I manage to stutter, "Mandy, Alvin – I think I found her."

Alvin finds a blanket in the rear compartment of one of the trucks and drapes it around her shoulders. Mandy doesn't stop looking at her, instilled with an unusual sense of fascination. The blue eyed girl sweeps her eyes between us, a neutral expression on her face though coupled with a sliver of curiosity. She doesn't speak.

"Are you okay?" I ask between stares. "Did they hurt you at all?" The sickness has since abated.

She shakes her head and continues to look between us, refusing to make a sound.

"What are we supposed to do now?" Mandy cuts in.

Alvin stands up from his squatting position and looks around the bay. "Well, we can't stay here. Ulrich said we should get her out, hide her for awhile; possibly take her to Enoch."

"Do you know why they want to kill you?" I ask while attempting to capture her attention.

The girl nods and lifts a finger apathetically towards the direction of the Narthex. She continues to look around the room, as if the topic of conversation doesn't interest her. I find myself captivated by every move she makes, the shifting of her eye, the rising in her chest, as if drawn to her like some unnatural flame. At times she tries to speak, but each time she inhales and parts her lips, something else captivates her attention and stops as if her sentence was forgotten. The more I watch her, the more I can't reason why anyone would cause her harm, and though as magnificent of a creature as she is, it will not be long before they find her. It takes all my will to pull away.

"Alvin – Can you get one of the trucks up and running? We need to get her as far away from here as possible."

"I think the old Ford has some go in her yet."

I stop him before he starts off. I take the girls hand, immediately capturing her direct, though waning, attention. "Go with Alvin, he'll protect you as best as he can. Stay in the truck, you're safer there." I point her towards him, just in case her reality is having trouble sorting itself out. She looks at me fondly, reaching out with her opposite hand and poking at my cheek as if it were a mirage.

"Alvin?" My tone is enough to carry the plea for help.

"I got her." He intercedes between us and takes up her hand to lead her toward the run down Ford.

She adopts a confused look and her face is torn with concern.

"Don't worry." I say as I manage to my feet. "You'll be all right."

As soon as they are on their way, I turn and find Mandy staring at her own finger and crossing her eyes as she pokes herself in the nose. She giggles.

"Funny." I fall in love with her. "How do we open the rear doors?"

"They're magnetically sealed, but there's a switch." She grabs my hand. "Come on, I'll show you where."

We rush to the exit, our boots echoing with a solid clank against the steel flooring. Mandy stops just short of the control panel, ducks into a walk-in cargo container, only then to emerge with a few down filled coats. "I'm not going out there in my underwear. It's cold out there."

I grab one from her, realizing that it's still fairly early and that the sun has yet to warm the horizon.

Together we reach the consul and together we hit the

button that releases the back doors. In a thunderous clamor of twirling gears the doors slowly part, sending echoes rumbling through the Mastodon. I see Alvin helping the girl into the truck and shutting the door behind her and then rounding to the passenger side. I am then swept up in the frigid air, and after a loud shiver, I catch Mandy's nipples poking through her thermal wear before she zips up her coat. She cocks her head and beams at me.

Once inside, Alvin tries to start the old beater, forcing fuel into the engine. The vehicle refuses to turn over.

Mandy starts jumping in place. "Come on, come on!"

After the third try the vehicle revs and exhaust spills into the bay. The excitement of our escape erodes from my face as I catch a pulse-rifle leveling at our position. "Get down!" I scream as I grab Mandy by the coat and throw my weight into her. A pulse scorches overhead, leaving behind the scent of ozone. The two of us scramble to get behind cover, just as a couple Pulse Energy Projectiles slam into the front end and windshield of the truck. Glass spews onto the floor, I am gored by a sinking feeling that either Alvin or the woman had been hit. That is until I hear Alvin screaming, "Enough already! I'm done."

The passenger side door is wide open.

"There she goes!" Someone shouts. But before I can discern her location, I am yanked by my collar by the naked albino. She drags both Mandy and I through the door, just as a round of blasts dent the neighboring equipment.

The woman helps us to our feet; ash and mud cling to our clothes. I don't know where we can run, there aren't any safe places. I run regardless. We all do. I can hear them chasing after us, their boots stomping against the ground, my breathing pouring from my lips as quickly as the flood of icy air fills them up again. My legs wobble due to the uneven terrain and I do everything I can not to trip. It's not until our course lines up with the foreboding shadow in the distance, that I realize that the girl is leading us towards the ruins of the

115

Narthex.

I hear men shouting from the side ramp of the Mastodon as a few more of the crew joins in the pursuit. I recognize a them, the blonde from the kitchen, Jenson and Reynolds, and a few others from the vestibule before the rains. They are all coming after us, setting aside their weapons to do us in by hand.

When Mandy is grabbed by the back of her hair, that's all it takes before I turn around and slug him in the mouth. It is then that I understand the full direness of my mistake when the rest descend upon me. I scream for Mandy to run but it's too late, they take her as well and drag us both to the ground. I'm kicked in my stomach, a fist at the back of my head, while my coat is ripped as I'm thrown from one end to the other. Mandy is struck as well, her hair pulled back while another jabs her in the chest. We are thrown together, surrounded by a mob of people, a blend of fists, elbows, and legs! I throw ash into our assailants' eyes, and kick another in the face, but every effort returns another in kind. I struggle until my legs are crippled with pain, a taste of iron trickling from both my nose and mouth. It isn't long, as I lose strength in my limbs - barely enough to bring them to deflect the next attack - that we're defeated.

My mind flashes with the event from the previous day, until a PEP whirls overhead, striking a man in the face and throwing him fifteen feet from where he once stood.

Another taste of ozone jets through the crew and this time turning him over-end and head first onto the desert floor; those remaining freeze in place. I catch sight of the sniper mid-ramp of the Mastodon with Ulrich at her side. "No body better fucking move!"

I peer between the cracks of bodies as the albino continues her flight with a few men in pursuit, too far to realize the situation behind them. I watch as she ducks into the opened gash, disappearing into the darkness of the Narthex, like a phantom to the grave.

Her would-be assassins slow their speeds and then halt entirely as if catching sight of the freakish horror of the place; paralyzed in fear of what lay beyond. They back up, one foot at a time, though I've no reason to understand why, until a moment passes and see it! Beneath the raising of the sun, as tiny rays filter through the tar-pitched sky, and bend the horrid shadows of the like-spires of the tenebrous citadel – reaching out like some undue horror to envelope the entire compound - a figure blazes in the refraction of light, a man of stance and elegant height, with white hair that drizzles down to the length of his waist, eyes of deep set purples and sunken sockets, emerges from the veil of darkness, across its portal, and into our world.

Then the others appear, two at first, a variety of sizes and manner, materializing from the ships interior, beaming in their gaunt, though candid, repertoire of expression. Four then five at first, then nine and ten, thirteen! Thirteen in all! All giants in their human heights, each glistening with a little portion of the sun as it caresses their unclothed bodies. Time seems amiss, retreating to a slower pace, as we exchange glances between the newcomers, plagued by both awe and confusion; all hostilities forgotten as by some unspoken armistice. The first to emerge sings:

"Glory be and behold! I am Aramos Lyciel – returned from our heavenly sojourn, come to rejoin our place amidst the company of man!"

Luce leans against an exposed track of the Mastodon, glaring at the spectacle before her with hate in her eyes. I cannot imagine the thoughts that boil inside her but whatever it is I fear will consume her. Her eyes narrow and rise amidst the weaving of thoughts whilst her lips every-so-often curl up into a sneer. She's too far from the rest to be much of a bother but enough to cause me worry – on top of everything else that is.

Laughter spills across the landscape, as both crews

mingle between one another: the pallid women leaning against the men, whispering private things into their ears, as the pasty men lavish their attentions upon the women, and even the occasional same-sex flirting and smiling between one another. A few bottles of the Mastodon's finest liquors have been brought out to share with their newly found friends. Even Mandy has found one who introduced himself to us and proved to be enchanting – I for one could find no malintent.

I sit off, perplexed by the entire scheme of events as Dr. Reins swabs a few ointments on my wounds, bandaging me up for the second time since I've been here. And although the esteemed physician is blind, his eyes no longer the focus of his soul, his expression of concern and befuddlement sheds wrinkles across his brow, a good indication that he too finds something troubling about the arrival of the remnant crew.

"What's with the look?" I ask as he pinches a gash on my arm that causes me to wince in pain.

He sighs, never halting from his work and retorts. "Mr. Burbank, doctors pride themselves on keeping their patients ailments secret and although sacred as it is, I find no regret in betraying it now, if indeed you promise to do me the favor and keep this to yourself."

I nod my head, hoping that his sensors will pick up the motion as a confirmed "yes".

"They are not albino's Mr. Burbanks and although human as they look, I do not believe that there is anything human about them."

His words somehow frighten me, as if the declaration in itself opened the doors to my imagination and that my subconscious now searches for the worst possible match. But there they are, bustling about the camp as if human, talking and walking like humans; laughing like humans. Perhaps it is their skin or their lack of shame that has the doctor so spooked, or is it the spell they cast over the earth-movers that has him preaching about creatures from outer space.

I try to reason it. "Who knows what they've been into?

Maybe they had to engineer a serum to enable them to survive a hostile environment and it went all wrong? Genetic defects have been known to happen, I'm sure the Line has reports full of such abnormalities." It is only after I say this that I am struck by a leaf of doubt.

Seiger just shakes his head and mutters, "They're too perfect to be a mistake." He tightens the last bandage. "Good as new, now you'll match your earlier wound."

I get up off the alumiplast crates we've been using as a makeshift examination table, my muscles descend into a painful outcry as my wounds call out from beneath their bandages. I stifle a yelp before saying beneath the clenching of my jaw, "Thanks Dr. Reins. I appreciate it."

His voice grows serious. "Remember what you promised," I stare into those gleaming red optics of his, "Not a word." There is something haunting about him, like a man possessed by some dire spirit, bringing tides of ill-omen. It means that much to him.

I nod and wave as I make my way toward Luce, knowing with nervous paranoia that I am the focus in his field of vision. I keep walking just the same, regardless that I can feel the red tracers on my back - like harbingers of doom.

Despite a lack of change in her stance, Lucile opens up the conversation before I even get a chance. "How are the wounds, Harmon?"

"Not as bad as they could have been." I lean up against the tracks, mimicking her stance, trying hard not to come across as mocking. "Thanks to you."

She humphs, allowing a tiny bridge-of-a-smile to creep across her cheek. "Don't take this personal but I need to protect my investments. I'm sure I'm up a couple thousand for hazard pay. The ERR isn't going to appreciate the added sum. Besides..." She stares out across the desert. "I like having you around." If I didn't know better, I'd say she is softening up to me.

I chuckle lightly, feeling good that I brought some

change in her expression. "It seems that everything turned out in the end hasn't it? I couldn't believe when Aramos declared that they were willing to share the profits of the Narthex's recycling, even taking a smaller cut. From what I gather, that's enough for everyone to purchase a ticket with a little left over."

What slice of happiness I brought her only vanishes into the cruelty of her face.

"And leaving them just shy? I'll believe that when I have the credits in my account. No one's that generous." She brings a leg up to steady her lean against the tracks, which reveals the dismal stock of her rifle resting beside her. "You may disillusion yourself with thoughts that everything is okay but the winds are stirring and I can still taste copper in my mouth." She takes the pack of cigarettes out of her coat pocket and slides one into her mouth, brings out the lazer lighter, slips the stick into it's open chamber, and retracts it lit – smoke rolling from her lips. "It's coming Harmon, you just don't see it yet–"

Her mouth closes tightly around the tube in her mouth as her attentions bleed to something over my shoulder. When I turn to look, I am startled to see the ashen shape of Aramos, just an arms length away, tucked tightly in a few spare clothes and white coat.

"I apologize for interrupting your conversation. I do not wish to intrude, but I hadn't the opportunity to make either of your acquaintance and thought by some chance, you would be kind enough to make my own." He softly curls his lips to make a smile. He faintly smells of lavender. The albino extends his hand out to me. "I am Aramos."

I take up his hand but find it disturbingly cold. When he notices my discomfort he retracts his grip. "Poor circulation – it only serves me in space, I'm afraid."

I shake my head to dissuade any thoughts of offense. "It's all right. I should have remembered that about you from your other crew member."

"Yes, I wanted to thank you for taking wounds in her stead. We are frail creatures. Seima doesn't speak a word, but ah," he breathes in from a taste of memory. "You should hear her sing."

"Was there something you wanted, Aramos?" Luce talks from the end of her cigarette, now standing as if ready for a fight.

Aramos only smiles. "Lucile Callaghan isn't it? Your people speak highly of you. I only wanted to discuss the process of recycling the Narthex."

"Have you changed your mind?" she combats.

"On the contrary, from what I have gathered it's Mr. Burbanks here who will appraise the ship. Then once the figures are completed, you'll send for a pilot crew to dismantle it and arrange for payment, am I correct?"

"Sounds like you have it right." She crosses her arms with impatience.

"Afterwards, what will happen to us once the ships drop in?"

"Personally, I don't give a damn. We'll hand you over to Enoch officials and let them deal with you."

"I see." I expect a change in facial features, perhaps showing some form of worry or distrust, but Aramos continues in good spirits. "Perhaps you won't mind if I accompany Mr. Burbanks during his appraisals, help him through the ship so we may speed up this process."

"Like I said," she throws her cigarette on the ground, spewing her last cloud of smoke. "I don't care what you do. Just don't get in the way of his job… or ours." She slings the Luftgung onto her shoulder and looks to me. "I've got letters to write." She turns and walks toward the Mastodon's side ramp.

Both Aramos and I watch her go before he springs, "There are those who were never meant to be happy, and then those who never allow themselves to be happy. Sometimes it's difficult to distinguish between the two and oftentimes they are one in the same." He looks down at me from his 6 foot height, his platinum spun hair curving about his face like a sickle and grins. "Well, hello Seima."

I spin around and find the pale beauty leaning against the set of tracks just shy a few inches, her hand already poised to stroke my hair and run down my cheek. Her bluish eyes glisten with a softness I could never compare. "You'll have to excuse her Mr. Burbanks, as she's a very affectionate girl. And from my understandings is smitten with both you and Miss Khaldolen for your courage earlier. I'm afraid it'll prove difficult to be rid of her." Seima kisses the side of my lip, her touch is like frost on a glass but powerful enough to send shivers racing down my vertebrae. "There now," Aramos eyes darken as they narrow within his bruised appearing sockets. "Aren't we friends?"

Alvin cracks another glowrod, painting the room in a yellow cast. He wipes the bristles of his chin, having not the chance to shave since the previous day. From my understanding, he hasn't slept either.

Mandy scuffles closer to me in order to place some distance between the prowling Seima, who takes an interest in every move we make. The whole "feeling" that Lucile was talking about now plays its hand against me. While Aramos insists that their presence is a benefit, I cannot help but feel that they are spying on us. Silence has been the better, though tense, portion of our journey. I've come down with a touch of the shakes, constantly looking over my shoulder to see what the ghostly duo are keeping themselves to, only to catch them looking at me from time to time. I now fear that there is something hidden beneath those Cheshire grins of theirs. Perhaps this is why Ulrich decided to send Alvin with us, though from what I hear, he volunteered. It doesn't help matters that this is the first time I've seen him with a gun.

Mandy reacts to some face she sees over her shoulder and stuffs her arm beneath mine, grabbing hold of my shoulder as best as she can without throwing off her balance. The silence between us finally gets to me. "Aramos?" My voice flutters through the death of the ship like a moth. "There's something that's been bothering me since we first found the Narthex..."

His tenor voice cuts in from behind me and I can imagine his aristocratic walk, stiff back, drawn head, and his hands crossed behind him. "Yes?"

"Whatever happened to the Narthex those many years ago? That is, when you left Earth?"

He pauses as if needing the right breath to answer. "There was a fire. It started because of faulty wiring. It spread through the ship like a windswept inferno. It found its way into the oxygen and there were explosions."

I stop as the footsteps behind me end. I realize then that Seima has attached herself to a nearby railing, clutching at it for support, staring off into the darkness of the ship; remembering. Aramos drops a hand of compassion against her shoulder before continuing. "Many of us were burned alive and others suffocated from the depressurization, some simply from the smoke."

He places his hand against the cold gritty steel of a nearby wall. "The walls were so hot that they would scold your flesh and in some areas your lungs would ignite from the heat. Only a few of us survived. When all was finally cooled, we found ourselves adrift in space, far beyond our intended course, with no hope of ever reaching Alpha Centauri or returning home. And so, flung aimlessly through the void, we drew straws – with the shortest keeping watch while the rest of us were put in hibernation. It was the only way we were able to survive."

"But..." Mandy's shrunken voice rises out of hiding, "How long did he or she have to watch over you?"

"A long time. His sacrifice gave us a second chance." His fingers retract from the wall as if it had been beneath some arduous weight.

"What happened to him?" Mandy begs with a tear of sympathy.

"He inevitably went mad. We forced him into hibernation until such a time he could be cured. We will take him with us into Enoch when the time comes."

"If you don't mind me asking, Mr. Aramos, but how is it that you all came to be what you are now?" Alvin asks.

He looks us all dead in the eye. "In the blackness of space, there are things in which there is no defense. Our condition was the only means available to ensure our survival. I don't want to speak any more on this."

"But how did you get back home?" Mandy asks inquisitively, while swallowing with the fear of crossing to far into the unknown. "So far off course?

He rubs the wall and finally, his arm exerted as if by the weight of eighty years, drops it to his side and says. "Luck." But he is no longer with us, too far engrained in memories past.

As much as I once feared them, I hold nothing but pity. And although stricken with the desire to welcome them into the folds of humanity, embrace them as brother and sister, I am held by my doubts and suspicions. For how beautiful they are, I find them foreign; for how noble they be, I find them frightening; though how moved I am, I am stalled.

Silence once again reclaims the interior of the Narthex and for a slight instance I swear that I can hear the sound of tears dropping solemnly onto the merciless cold of steel.

I ponder the shape of the armillary sphere on a seconds break before uploading the day's figures onto a dataplate. I hand them off to Luce and she in turn hands them off to Ulrich.

He scrolls through the estimates, shaking his head and then catches the bottom number. "Exactly what I thought." He returns the plate in kind. "Doesn't mean a damn thing to me."

"Don't worry. It's just good to have a general idea of what the drop pilots will take and then a comparison note to what the recyclers will get out of it. If we're within the ballpark then there isn't anything to worry about. If you're down a good percent... well, they'll have to investigate which is a long and grueling process. Trust me – I want to be as close as possible."

Luce slides the plate back to me. "Where's Aramos, Harmon? Not out seducing any of my workers, I suspect?"

"He said he had to tend to some of his people. He wasn't very specific in his mentioning, but assured me that there's nothing to be worried about."

"There's nothing that he does that doesn't concern me." She slides the plastic off another pack of cigarettes as natural as a snake sheds its skin. "Don't be taken in by their innocence. There are a lot of things unaccounted for."

I press a few buttons on my ALC to review what sections I had touched in comparison to those that I still need to assess. "Such as?"

"How they became this way for starters. They were human once but now they've become as they have, and you cannot convince me for a second that whatever transformation they've undergone hasn't played some trick against their mind."

She was beginning to anger me for reasons I do not know why. "All they've been wanting is to return home and be among their own kind." I just can't see why they couldn't leave well enough alone.

"I don't think you noticed at all, Harmon, but they don't have a kind anymore. So they want to be with people then what?" She lights a cigarette with her lazer-lighter before continuing, "...live out the rest of their days reveling in our company? I think not. Earth is a barren rock Harmon and it's becoming more barren by the day. The day of green fields and pretty flowers has come to its end, volcanoes are spewing more carbon and sulpher dioxide into our atmosphere every month, and you expect these things to go without hope of joining the rest of us on Alpha Centauri when there's no more oxygen to breathe? It'll take them a lifetime to collect enough credits to book passage for all of them."

Ulrich clears his throat. "I'm sorry to say Harmon but Luce's got a point. They would have to be idiots to just hand over their share to us. More likely, it was a false-promise designed to satisfy the mob. Give them the upper hand and I'm sure the tables will turn."

I'm about to tell them both how wrong they are but I am interrupted at the flap to the tent is thrown aside and Mandy hastily bounds in. "Luce... Ulrich..." Her face is covered in smears of grease. She drops her hands onto her knees and stoops to regain her breath. "We have five tracks missing off the front rotary and three in the rear. It looks like sabotage. We're dead in the ash!"

Luce's face scrunches in outrage. "Who!?" She tosses her cigarette to the side and grabs Mandy by the shoulders. "Was it that pale piece of shit, Aramos? Was it any of the Narthex crew?"

"I... I don't know Luce." Mandy looks like a frightened child facing against a behemoth. "I just found it that way."

All of our heads snap as Alvin rushes in. "We've got trouble."

The metallic beast sits atop a distant hill, a speck against the gray of the sky. Lucile passes a spotting scope to me after getting her fill, and I'm able to see the thing as clearly, the M113 transport. I thought we had seen the last of it. I hand off the scope to Mandy.

"Bloody bastards," Ulrich spits. "Looks like that black-toothed bastard can't take 'no' for an answer."

"What are they doing out there?" I ask

Luce checks her Luftgung's energy pack. "Causing problems, that's what they're doing. No one sneaks into my camp and fucks with my equipment!"

Mandy finishes wiping some of the grease off her face and stuffs the rag into her belt. "I don't see what they hope to accomplish out there, there's what? Four of them?"

"That Raus character could have gone back for some help with promises of a share in the Narthex. I wouldn't put it passed him. I'm surprised the whole sector hasn't descended on us – bee's and their honey and all." Alvin gets his chance to look through the scope, watching as they had probably been doing to us. "Oh – that's not good."

"What is it Alvin?" Ulrich asks as he checks his Styllus.

"They have a 50 cal strapped to the top of it."

"Looks like their just waiting for their opportunity." Ulrich says bitterly.

"Should I be worried?" Mandy asks with a couple fingers hanging out of her mouth.

"Cartridges the length of your hand; capable of cutting you in half in an instance."

Mandy's eyes widen and she trembles at Ulrich's words. All right, I'm going to hide inside the Mastodon. Let me know how things turn out."

"Unfortunately, the rest of us don't get that luxury." Lucile announces, "Mandy needs to get those treads repaired as soon as possible, which means I can't have her risking her life on this one." Luce runs her fingers through her blood-red hair and sighs, "I hate to ask this of you Harmon, but this is the only circle of people that I trust. For all we know those junk-rats may have some friends in our camp, best not involve too many people. I need you to go with us and cut these bastards down as quickly as possible. If they get here with that beastie of theirs, no one is safe. Are you with us?"

Everyone's eyes are on me, all waiting for an answer. I can't believe this. I'm no soldier but the alternative frightens. For one, I could be pulverized beneath a rain of bullets and PEPs assaulting that thing, where the same could happen if I stayed here. This isn't what I was hired for. But she's right, no one's safe anymore, not even Mandy.

My chest starts to pain me as I nod my head in agreement.

"Then it's settled then, the four of us will make our way to the transport and flank it from both sides. We can catch them by surprise! They'll never see us coming." Luce pauses for a short moment, glancing over her shoulder after having noticed a white shape stroll passed her peripheral.

I follow her gaze and to a member of the Narthex crew. "On second thought..." She turns up a sneer, "I should stay here and keep my eye on things." She takes a deep breath and grinds her teeth, "I'll take roost atop the Mastodon in case they make it past you. I've got to stay behind and make sure these pricks don't try anything."

Ulrich and Alvin just nod and pick up a few rifles previously confiscated from the laboring crew. Mandy rushes over to me and hugs me around the waist. "You come back, okay? No funny business. Just do what you have to do and stay safe."

I hug her back, and kiss the top of her head. I can't help but feel something disquieting settle within my bones. And as I look just over top the softness of Mandy's brown hairs, I see the deep bruises and glowing blues of Seima's eyes as she decadently leans against the Mastodon's tracks, watching from afar.

She moves as if usurped by my notice, inevitably forced to stroll back towards the Narthex without a second glance.

Ulrich takes to the front, sneaking around rocks, hills and rubble. Alvin stays close to my side, keeping his weapon pressed against his shoulder with a stern look I've never seen in him before. We've made our way carefully and as timely as few men are capable of on foot. I'm astounded by my ability to keep up, perhaps inspired by the fear of being left behind or being caught alone. I remember back to the old World War 2 movies I used to watch off the Line, and how dangerous getting in front of the barrel to a M2 50 caliber machine gun was: the spray of bullets, and the barbaric mutilation it wreaks against a person's body – all 128 lbs of pure devastation. I am glad the most of the world had adopted a more civilized means of warfare. At least a PEP isn't invasive, it just shocks the body to death.

The way that both Alvin and Ulrich move together makes me question whether they have done this sort of thing before.

My chest stabs with fright when Ulrich brings up his hand to halt our progress. He crawls up a steep slope to an adjoining hill face, one adjacent to the M113, just a few hundred feet from its position. He motions for us to join him quietly.

When Alvin and I reach the plateau, Ulrich nods just over the point. I poke my head out into the open, just enough to catch view of the surrounding area. The place looks empty. Not a single guard traverses the area, nor do I hear anything beyond my own stifling breath. None of this makes any sense, though I'm no tactical expert, but why would they leave their vehicle on a hill were it could be easily spotted? I squeeze the handle to the Derringer-198, a 9 lbs short stock pulse-rifle that was given to me by Ulrich before we left. It feels awkward in my hands. Something about this whole affair unnerves me, beyond the initial nausea that settles in when one expects to have to kill someone. Something's not right and from what I could tell, Alvin and Ulrich feel it too.

As luck would have it, the machinegun isn't manned, which only makes things easier. We wait a short while, expecting at any moment for a noise or even one of Raus' cohorts to pop out from somewhere, but nothing. Everything is still, nothing moves. Ulrich finally takes a chance, and hoists himself to his feet and starts a stealthy approach toward the vehicle, his gun shifting from one side to the other. Alvin and I keep our weapons out, in the case Ulrich is fired upon. After thirty feet or so, he motions for the both of us to follow.

My heart rams the inside of my chest, and my throat seizes itself in a tight grip that barely affords me air to keep the balance on my weapon. I hear nothing save the pounding in my ears, and feel nothing save the weight of the rifle. As we get closer to the transport, I am taken up by that all too familiar scent mixed with a tinge of copper. Once we reach the base of the dreaded machine, the smell only gets worse. It's when we reach the backside when my heart stops entirely.

Lain strewn across the ground in a pond of blood and carnage, lay the eviscerated remains of 9 human beings, all piled top of each other, completely stripped of all possessions and clothing. The sight makes me real, and I expel what little contents I have in my stomach out and onto the desert floor. The smell – that horrible smell! – thrusts itself into my nostrils and I cannot stop myself from dry heaving, feeling dizzy from the thickness in the air. I have troubles breathing, and after quickly clearing my mouth from the taste of acid, I cover my face with the ventilator, silencing my senses for my own good.

Alvin examines a pile of weapons next to the rear ramp, along side it is another pile of miscellaneous metallic things: watches, pins, buttons, fillings, rings, buckles, and the like. Their clothes had been torn to shreds and discarded in a pile of their own, just a few feet from the bodies that once wore them.

Ulrich examines the ground and surveys the scope of the terrain muttering, "They didn't fire a single shot."

Alvin stares with a morbid fascination at the mound of corpses. "It's like they were ripped apart by something—"

The words lunge out of me, "Not human."

The three of us exchange a look that only comes during a shared realization when past and present events finally unveil the true terror.

"Get in the APC!" Ulrich barks while jumping to his feet, "We need to get back to the encampment!"

Alvin pilots the beast into the heart of the camp, while

Ulrich keeps an eye down the long barrel of the antique weapon. Where once the camp was bustling with activity, it is now deserted. There are no signs of struggle, no points of scarring or disruption, but only the sounds of the wind filtering through the organ-like vessel that is the Narthex. I share the front porthole with Alvin, the two of us searching for something that would indicate what had happened.

Ulrich slides out of the top port to join us. He pulls out his Styllus and hands me back the Derringer. "Alvin, I want you to drive this thing to the edge of the camp and keep out of sight. Man that M2 if there's any trouble and keep this thing running. Mr. Burbanks and I will go in and see where everyone went. Do not leave without us, Alvin. I'm counting on you to get us out of here."

He nods while placing his weapon next to him, "I wouldn't dream of it."

Ulrich drops the back hatch and I follow him out into the cold of the approaching night. Together, the two us make our way slowly towards the gapping maw of the black carrak. The whole encampment bleeds the same sinister feeling as I encountered while standing outside the Narthex the previous day - that gross feeling of apprehension. At times the shadows appear as if they shimmer, slowly shifting before my eyes. Even the crippled Mastodon has adopted a dreadful visage, torn as it is in its current state, billowing with the fear of the unknown.

I cannot help but feel small in the presence of the relic ship. It's damaged hull and crushed subsections only aid in the feeling of entropy that grips at my soul. And though as much as reason would suggest otherwise, telling me to run and never look back, I cannot help but feel drawn to the dark citadel that stands at the opposite end of the camp. And once we reach its threshold, Ulrich and I are lured passed its boundaries and into the darkness of its vacant corridors, followed by a cloak of uncertainty and death.

I turn on the flashlight of my ALC and keep the light as

a steady beam ahead of us. I take the lead, having memorized its layout due to my past ventures. My heart skips each time my boot scuffs against the texture steel, worried that it would attract those who live in the memories of this ship. As we move from room to room, sweeping each niche, I catch fleeting wisps fluttering from the luminance of the light, each dodging round corners like maddened fireflies. I can smell the horrid stench that seems to protrude from the very vessel itself, like the interior of a rotten womb.

In time, we reach a place I've been long avoiding, the central free-floating shaft that connects to the upper-chambers. At its bottom is an orange grease-stained jumpsuit. I pick it up and shuffle through it, frantically searching for blood or anything to indicate a struggle, but there is nothing. It is as if it was unzipped and fell from her shoulders in a single motion. The stone that has been accumulating in my stomach only grows larger. I look up into the darkness above and wonder what has become of her.

I shine my light into the dark tube, capable of only piercing the first 20 feet, before it dwindles into oblivion. There are a few foot holds here and there, but otherwise prove difficult to climb and if I were to fall... I don't have much of a choice.

Without a word, I hand the rifle to Ulrich, determined to climb to its very reaches in order to save whoever I can.

Ulrich holsters his gun, takes off his belt, and hands it to me. "You're going to need this up there." He whispers. I nod while putting on the holster, as he pats my shoulder. "You've done more than I've ever expected out of anyone. You're a good man, Harmon. I wish more people could be like you."

Before I'm able to respond, he intertwines his fingers and boosts me up to the first handhold. In order for me to reach the rest, I have to climb atop his shoulders and kick off of his hands. I hear him give a fleeting "good luck" before vanishing in the dark beneath me.

I struggle; pulling myself up by my fingertips in some spots, with mere inches for my feet. My hands strain against the weight of my own body as I tackle the next set of inlets, one after another. At times I feel like something presses against my shoulders, pushing me down and off into the darkness below. I struggle not to look. As I claw my way up, I fixate on the night Mandy and I shared together, feeling that moment, and knowing what it was to understand life beyond the fringes of Enoch; to know the hardships, to bleed, to cry and laugh with those constantly beneath the blade of ends. I focus on what she smells like, her combination of perfume, grease and lubricant. All this comes to me while climbing now 40 feet above the ground, giving me the confidence and courage to force myself upwards.

Then, I hear a harmonious melody sung by a gifted alto. It flows with a dramatic inspiration, like a siren's song, calling me out to sea. A dim orange glow appears above, luring me closer to its ledge, and up into a room. My head swims as one tends from waking out of a dream, and the room vanishes to the familiar meadow of Alpha Centauri. Children's laughter springs from the adjacent hillsides and buttermoths flutter by my face, brushing their silky wings across my cheek before flying off toward the clear blue sky.

"Welcome home, husband." Comes a vibrant voice behind me. Turning, I catch the gorgeous locks of a blonde woman, with eyes glowing the color of sapphires. She wraps her arms around my neck and pushes her slim form against my body. "I've missed you."

She leans closer into me, her lips falling onto mine and I'm stunned by the bleak coldness that bites into my mouth. The vision disintegrates into mere figments of shadow, before I'm returned to the desolate chambers of the ship – my lips in forced kiss to the waxy Seima.

I push us apart, stumbling backwards over a jumble of exposed wires that crackle and spark; barely lighting the floor-embedded fluorescents that bath the room in the color of a tarnished autumn leaf. Scrambling for the Stylus, I wrench it from its holdings and point it at her, shaking in remembrance of Raus and his crew. I unlock the safety, hear the powering of the battery cells and tighten my finger round the trigger, and in all this she simply looks at me from the warmth of her coat – a very human look that conveys the pain of the heart.

In her platinum strands, her anemic skin, and enchanting blues, she stands unopposed for me to strike her down in a barrage of energy blasts. As my hands tremble beneath the weight of the weapon, I happen upon the thought that she is innocent in all this, a victim amidst the turmoil of this nightmare. And in doing so, I find myself lowering Ulrick's gun, returning it to its holster, as she crouches down to eye-level just a few feet away.

"Where is Mandy?" I ask desperately as I scrounge for my feet.

Seima just stares, succumbing to some dumbfounded trance, falling in love with the shine on a buckle or the shape of my hair. She reaches for my face with her outstretched fingers but I intercept them, hoping to gain her concentration. "Where's Lucile?"

Her lips part. "Not to worry, she's here."

She points with her pale fingers in the direction behind me and follows, for a short while, with her eyes. I grab her frigid hand and pull the both of us to our feet.

"Where?!" I demand while grabbing her shoulders. "Where are they? I need to find them!"

She steps back, allowing my hands to drop into hers and tugs me forward, "I'll show you."

I keep in contact, my hand clasped in her palm and give into the chilling numbness of her temperature. Together we follow the path of faint luminance, ducking beneath fallen ducts and steel beams. I worry that she's leading me to the rest of them, to fall victim to whatever horrors lay in wait. I keep a hand on the Styllus as my mind outlines their false forms in the hidden recesses, a place where no light resides.

I'm led onto the old pilot's bridge, a place cleared of the antiquated consuls, where deep scratches and missing floor panels now mark their place. I am overwhelmed by the horrid smell, a sickly combination of something that was burned, mixed with the ever pungent scent of decay, rust, sweat and sex. I cannot describe it anymore, as it is a combination of all these things, simultaneously stimulating my nose in a spiral of nausea, pain and pleasure. I'm about ready to turn back, my hand clasped over my nostrils until Seima pulls me farther.

The interior is shaped like a dome, one of multiple levels, of engineered steel cat-walks and upright hibernation tubes. We pass gruesome piles, some of miscellaneous metal knick-knacks, whilst others of torn garments and broken weapons. She takes me to the other end of the room, where laid at the very base of the center hibernation pod is Lucile's broken Luftgung, laying in pieces on the floor.

I rush towards it in a fit of desperation, prying at the hatch with my fingers, straining to find how it opens, all the while Seima cocks her head and examines me with a curious expression.

"God damn it! Fucking help me!" I scream as I bite into my lip as I struggle to push harder against the impenetrable lid.

She walks casually up to me, unconcerned by the strain in my muscles. Rounding to the other side, she unhooks a hidden latch that sends the lid flying to its farthest hinge, and me sprawling backwards onto the ground. A hiss erupts, and as the heavy fog of chilled nitrogen dissipates into the room, the unconscious form of Lucile is revealed from the casket of frost. She stands there, held in the receptacle by magnetic strips, her unveiled skin, face and breasts are taken to a pale blue; her crimson hair an enigma in the icy chamber. The light from my ALC shows hundreds of tiny ash colored dots staining her near perfect complexion. It isn't until I look closer, after the fog is fully lifted, that I realize the very nature of the discoloration - my God! they're cigarette burns. What have they done to you, Lucile? What have they done?

As I struggle to return to my feet, my fingers brush over something familiar. When I look to see what it is, I drain to the color of my companion, as I recognize the scarlet stained implants of the belated Dr. Seiger, glaring at me in a blank state of surprise! the batteries still giving off a fading glow. I stave off the invading thoughts of them being ripped from his temples whilst he was still alive. My chest throbs with the pains of terror and my limbs quake uncontrollably from the strain of the uncanny.

I get up and race toward the now open container. Beneath the cowl of urgency, I peel Luce from her prison, leaning her arctic body against mine. I take off my coat and drape it over her. The cold air of the early morning starts gnawing at my limbs.

"What are you doing?" Seima asks, while fiddling with her hair. "Where will you go?" Refusing to look at me as if hurt.

Her question flows through me like a spray of needles and I release what my mind is chanting over and over again. "I've got to get her out of here." I say as my teeth chatter. "We need to go before the rest show up."

"Why?" The question issues from her porcelain face.

I look at her, her features offer nothing save a façade of ignorance. I refuse to answer. It is after hoisting Lucile on my shoulders, carrying her as she had once carried Hendrix, I wonder what has become of my dear Mandy.

"Mandy is fine."

A lump forces itself into my throat as I realize that her lips didn't move. The words just came out of her, responding to how I'm thinking as if she's —

"Reading your mind?" She smiles, her burning sapphires following me, as I take a few steps backwards in aghast.

"Remember what you promised, husband." Her form

shifts and wavers, as if coming out of focus and then bending back again. "Not a word!"

I step farther and farther away, her figure blinks an inch to the side then back again. My brain starts to swivel, my body drowning in trepidation, my muscles lurching backwards on their own accord, I hear a voice welling from deep inside me, one of absolute authority and command, "RUN!"

Her form grows in stature without changing sizes. I am dwarfed beneath her presence, engulfed by her encroaching dominance. As my anxieties finally give into desperate panic, I follow my inner voice's advice and run.

"Let me know how things turn out." Laughter bursts from within my head, "No funny business!"

I race through the maze of wiring and back into the other room. I can feel Seima following behind me as my legs struggle from Lucile's weight. I can feel her nearing, as if floating just inches behind me. Everything slows as if I'm caught by some murky coil seized around my limbs and throat, squeezing and pulling me back into the inky blackness that waits behind. Ahead, I can see the central tube that descends below and suddenly realize that there's no way down! I'm beginning to wish I had thought this through.

Caught in the moment, I take a chance! Grabbing hold of a descending cable I wrap it around my arm, clutch hold of Lucile tightly, hold my breath and jump! – for an instant I can feel Seima's cold fingers forcing themselves through my hair as her laughter falls with us.

The fall is quick and I can hear the cable rending itself from the paneling above. The ship wails in anguish, as the sound of crashing metal and straining wire clamors all around me. I freefall for a few milliseconds, feeling the pressure of gravity seeping into my stomach before the dreaded jerk, the shifting of bone issuing a horrendous crack! hellish pain screaming through my body and the cabling rending into my arm, suspends my descent. I lose my grip on Lucile and as she falls, I take one swipe at her, catching her wrist as she grabs mine, but slips! My ALC tumbles down into the darkness and I catch her wide-eyed, now awake, expression as she follows the spiraling light into oblivion.

My arm is crushed beneath an invisible hand and I feel the familiar burn of frost spreading into my wounds. I scream as another grabs hold of my leg, another at my waist, and then another! They rip at my clothing, throwing fragments into the abyss, while pulling me upwards; their fingers burning into me like tiny embers of molten fire. I struggle against them, howling for them to let me go, but they force me higher into the heart of the ship.

My pants are forced from me, my shirt torn, is pulled freely from my struggling form. I thrash and screech but am stifled by the chill in the air. For awhile I feel as if I am flying, as a breeze flows forcefully over my skin. My mind fills with ancient portraits of demons, Incubus and Succubi carrying me off to the thralls of their satanic master. I cry out, my mind racing through prior calculations, integers and fractions: 9 lbs, 128, 112, 98, 3.5, 1.5, 3.6, 11 tons, 150 – no, 151! My entire life being sprawled out in a length of meaningless numbers as my flesh melts against the incursion of their touch! And when I find that my mind has overflowed, that my body has sustained far more than its share in torture – I cannot help but surrender to the darkness around me as I drift into the horrifying trenches of unconsciousness. It is then, I swear to you, the sensation of falling...

My head is cradled in a bare woman's lap, the smell of Anulla Roberts and lubricant is strong, mixed with a misplaced tinge of lavender. I open my eyes, still unable to see past the darkness around me. I try and move but my shoulder stabs at me with hatred.

I'm hushed by Mandy's familiar voice, "Try not to move, you dislocated your shoulder, along with a lot of other nastiness as well." She brushes the hair out of my eyes. "I told you to be careful."

For the moment, I am warm, though the chill of the textured steel is enough to indicate that I am fully naked. The strange thing is that I should be freezing right now.

"What happened?" I manage, as I settle back into her, the softness of her skin helps to sooth the pain.

"They brought you here. You must have passed out from the pain. They reset your shoulder. You're lucky nothing broke. What were you thinking?" I can barely make out her leafless silhouette in the dark.

I remember the devils carrying me through the air, Seima, and the mutilated forms of the old M113 crew. "I had to come back for you – had to save Luce. I couldn't leave you two here after what I found. Their faces!" I remember the pile of red. "Their bodies in pieces, thrown into a pile like discarded garbage. It was horrible, Mandy! I'm glad you didn't have to see it. The things they did – it wasn't human! Just wasn't human."

She shushes me softly and places a finger across my lips. "It'd be best if you didn't think about then. Look at the now. You're safe, Harmon. Everything is going to be all right." Her voice is as calming as the quiet hum of the oscillators in the city. She strokes her fingers through my hair and kisses my forehead, repeating herself, "Everything's all right."

In a screech of pain, my eyes are pierced by light drenching the central section of the Narthex bridge. Revealed is a hibernation pod, lying on it's back and stretched out like a sarcophagus, where atop stands the armillary sphere; reflecting ribbons of light against the walls. Raising my hand to douse the brilliant intrusion, I squint to perceive beyond the black that surrounds us, but find nothing save for discomforting shades of the unknown.

I ease myself to standing, ignoring the pain shooting through me, while holding my wounded arm close to my chest. Mandy doesn't object, instead opting to help me to my feet and support me as I shuffle closer to the ignited circle. Through the torment, I find myself at the foot of the hyber-pod, close enough to the sphere that I reach out and touch the copper rim, which sends it spinning in a slow celestial orbit. As it spins, so does my head, the world feeling as if I've tipped it into a dizzying rotation. I close my eyes to correct my vision, and when I open them again, I see an ethereal form radiating a profuse halo and crystal aura, walking counter-clockwise around the outside of the spotlight, never getting closer or further away, regardless that I'm standing still; spinning the room with every footfall.

"What a marvelous device, is it not? One could spend a lifetime pondering its quizzical shape and understanding the nature of its representation."

"Armos." I swallow, while grabbing hold of Mandy's waist, hoping it would slow the world. This must be a dream.

"A dream is it? No, Harmon you are not asleep, and yet you are not fully awake; caught somewhere between the veil of reality and the surreal. Isn't it wonderful, just the three of us?"

"You're a monster!" I yell before realizing the consequences.

"Monster!" He slams his palms onto the lid of the hiber-chamber, the world ceasing its spin for a mere second, before a simper passes his lips and he strolls the other way. "You think that because I've killed, that it makes me a monster? That I've gone through extravagant ends to ensure your safety, to protect you from people such as Raus, Jenson and Reynolds? You accuse me of being barbaric because I disemboweled them, where as they would feel no such mercy after drilling holes in you with their ancient weaponry. A monster you say? You should praise me as your savior."

My speech is fueled by the inhuman atrocities he's forced me to witness. "But what about Lucile? What did she ever do to deserve the torture you put her through?" I shout to him, not caring what happens and knowing full well that

I'm at their mercy.

He stops. "Sweet, honorable, caring – Luce. A woman after my own heart; she wasn't the first who found the Narthex. She arrived a few moments before a couple from division 8 beat her to the claim. Why did they deserve to have the Narthex, it was in her sector after all, they just happened to be in the right place, at the right time. It's too bad she had them assassinated and their bodies left for the rains to dissolve. Besides, who would know? And you call me barbaric! I at least take credit for what I do."

"You're lying!" My eyes water from the stress of it all.

"Mr. Burbanks, I don't have to lie, the truth is delectably more satisfying. How did Miss Callaghan put it, 'pretty damn lucky', I suppose. I found that Lucile enjoys making her own luck. As one would have it, she even had time orchestrate a revolt, using poor Hendrix's death as a means of inciting a mob against poor Seima. She could have stopped it at any time, but decided to intervene only when the two of you were threatened. How convenient for her. Very good indeed."

I shake my head in disbelief. I look at Mandy, who keeps straight faced – watching as the lights spin round.

"Harmon – you've been manipulated since you first arrived and yet you put more trust in those who have continually harmed you, and anger at the one person who's told you the truth."

I struggle to keep my balance as the room parades around me like a twisted carousel. I can't tell if he's lying, all I know is that I hate him. For everything that I've been put through, for everything he's made me see, I hate him. "Why?" I demand, "Why, me? Why tell me?"

"Because we chose you, Harmon! It doesn't get simpler than that! You come so highly recommended, after all. Because Seima chose you, because Mandy chose you, because Lucile and Ulrich and those previous to them chose you. If you knew what we have experienced, what we have seen, then you would understand why it is that we want, and what it is that we want in you. It is the same reason why I shall never let you go Harmon, why I'll never let Mandy go. Why I'll never rest until those like you will keep us company until the end of days." He throws himself into the radiance and off him reflects the heavenly constellations, born on the walls like a shadow lamp, "I have survived the fires of Tartarus and ventured beyond the threshold of dreams. I drifted into the bleakness of eternity and heard the whispers of the dark. I have seen the fate of man while gazing in the decayed eyes of the Lord of Spirits! I bring you immortality, a chance to sail the Solar Barque, to prey on those who would do you harm. I can give you everything you've ever dreamed! Give into me Harmon! Give into us! Surrender yourself into our embrace and we shall invest in you the secrets of Nod and the Earth shall harm you no more."

The ferocious boom of a heavy pulse-pistol wails overhead, striking Armos straight in the neck, and sending him across the room. The dome is filled with yellow effulgence as glowrods clamor across the floor.

"Mandy! Harmon!" Screams Ulrich as he pelts off a couple additional blasts from his Stylus toward the ceiling. Alvin and the hobbling Luce aren't far from him.

Mandy and I race towards them ducking beneath the keening of their weapons. Uncertain of what they're firing at, I look above me and see the scattering forms of the Narthex crew crawling across the ceiling and walls, climbing overtop the embedded bodies of the cloth-less dirt-movers, imprisoned in the unearthly metals of the ship's hull – spread like a demonic feast. The pale creatures drop to the ground to avoid the hail of PEPs, their forms gliding like spectres, skipping in and out of corporealness with white blurs following behind them like cloaks of satin.

As soon as we pass them, Lucile pulls back with us while Alvin and Ulrich stand between the coming onslaught. Pistol and rifle fire explodes behind us, along with the high-pitch screams of the Narthex Crew. The three of us continue through the hallway and once we reach the shaft, Lucile hands the two of us a harness, and helps to attach us to the tight line they must have used to climb up.

"Mandy, get your ass down there! I'll follow Harmon. Ulrich and Alvin should be coming shortly. Here," she hands over her rifle, "Cover the escape as best as you can!"

Mandy nods, shouldering the weapon on her bare skin, her teeth already giving into the cold. I could feel it as well – whatever it was that was keeping us warm is now leaving us, or perhaps we had left it. Mandy attaches the line to her harness and zips down the cabling without a word.

Luce shows me the proper means of securing the cord to the mag-pulley, I step into the harness that comes with it.

"It's magnetic, just squeeze the handle to slow your descent! Don't land too hard or you'll break your legs." She shoves a glowrod in my belt, "Now get down there!"

I nod unsure as she pushes me down into the darkness of the tube. I squeeze as hard as I can, sometimes halting completely, but loosening it slowly to make my way towards the bottom. Once I touch the ground, I pry myself free, and crack the glowrod against the ground. I spin round to find the corridors vacant. Mandy is no where to be found.

I hold up the light searching the area, my wounds make it difficult for me to hold it too high. At least my head is finally clearing up. My foot steps on something foreign, and when I look, I find the 38 that must have fallen with the rest of my clothes. I pick it up just as Luce zips down the line.

"She gone! Luce – Mandy is gone!" I yell as she unhooks herself from the cable.

"What?! I thought I told her to cover the exit, where the fuck did she run off to?"

"I don't know. I was right behind her."

"Son of bitch, she's got my fucking gun!" Luce screams as she throws her mag-pulley against the wall.

"I'll go look for her." I announce as I try for the south

hall.

Lucile grabs my good arm. "Are you out of your goddamn mind?!"

"I'm not leaving without her!" I scream.

She rears her hand back as if she plans to strike me, then grabs at her head and squeezes. "Fine! Five minutes and we're out of here – with or without you. I didn't risk my life just so you two can play hide and seek."

"I'll be all right." I say as I rush off cradling my shoulder into an adjoining hallway.

Above the turmoil she yells, "Just come back to me..." her voice dissipating in the echoes of the violence around us.

I pass through every corridor, running around each bend as if I've lived here my entire life. The dark shadows retreat to the glow of the chemical-light and it is as if the debris itself shifts to allow my passing. I can hear the sounds of gunfire echo around me, people screaming, voices yelling, but I drive it as far from my mind as I am able. In the small amount of time that I am allotted, I sweep a fair number of rooms and places that I would go had I decided to run and hide. After each area, I wonder whether she had instead rushed to the exit and that she is waiting there for me with everyone else. For some reason, I know it isn't true – a feeling that she hides somewhere near, watching me. I run in pain, a terrible seeping pain that bursts within me each time my lungs take air. I rush from corridor to corridor, dodging piles of rubble and fallen girders. It isn't until I reach the storage bay that I can smell that awful scent again.

The ground starts to shift from beneath me and the walls distance themselves beyond the reach of the yellow glow. I can hear the melodies of her voice, playing in the confines of my mind, altering my perceptions of the world around me. I steady myself against a storage crate, trying effortlessly to pierce beyond the dark realm that surrounds me. I can feel her breath against my neck, her hands now caressing my inner thigh, and climbing up my waist and to my chest.

"Oh – husband, where are you going? You must stay here forever. You cannot imagine how lonely I'd be."

I turn and swing at her with my left arm but she moves with it in dance.

"Have I made you angry, do I not make you happy?" Seima takes my arm and wraps it snuggly around her waist. She grabs at my face and kisses me savagely. "Please tell me what I must do to—"

The gun goes off.

Seima stares at me, as her eyes bleed white, her mouth opens and a scream racks the inside of my brain! a sound that makes the world quake without end, a blend of excruciating pain and sorrow, a sound so disturbing that my eyes shut out the vision around me, and my ears lie deaf to the sounds of firefight. Ringing bells, sirens blaring; pain, so much pain! the screaming never ceasing, wailing and wailing until that is all that exists!

I fire again, and again, each one killing me as if I were shooting myself! I push back with my legs, firing an additional time, but missing as she distorts her form, falls to the ground and starts thrashing against crates, tile and floor. I throw my hands to my ears to block out the noise, regardless that it will do no good!

I careen backwards, blinded by the noise in my skull, and scratch at the texture steel, feeling the pain as my fingernails peel from the cuticle. I writhe as if there is nothing more to this existence than pain. I realize that I have the power to end it all in one single action. I bring the gun to my head.

I am stopped by someone's hand and pulled to my feet. A tiny hand supports me round the waist as we run somewhere distant, where the sounds of Seima's death knell dwindles into nothingness. The darkness slowly creeps away and soon I am able to hear the sound of our feet plopping against the metal floor. Mandy keeps her arms tight around me but doesn't say a word. The firefight has ceased, no longer can the wail of the PEPs be heard, and the ship once again returns to a realm of silence.

We race through the empty hallways, passing beneath scores of thermal scarring left behind by our rescuers. My thoughts drift in and out about Seima, her huddled form curled in the fetal, left alone in the emptiness of the ship. I think about how it was to have been adrift in space, with nothing but the burden of dreams and fading memories as her only companions. I think only of screams, the one that tears now at my heart. I can still hear it echoing somewhere in my head as my subconscious struggles to bury it in a locked vault where all horrible things are left. She's not dead, as death would prove a compassionate mercy, but living in something worse than death – floating in the dismal place between dreams and the surreal, silent and alone, like Aramos, like the rest of the lost crew – all searching for something solid to hold onto.

I hardly notice as we pass over the trail of crimson or the wet slopping noise it makes as we run through it. It is only as we come across a mangled form, a bloodied wretch of a person, that we realize what it is, a figure mangled by fist and claw. And while we stoop over its broken form, it reaches for our ankles, calling from a blood choking sputter, "Don't leave me here, City Boy." Ulrich cries as he holds in a portion of his chest, "Here, is where I don't wish to die."

The three of us reach the opening in the Narthex's hull. Mandy and I support the fallen Ulrich on either side, pulling him as we go; his legs dragging behind us. Alvin rushes up to relieve us, grabbing him underarm and toward the exit.

I can hear the rumbling of the diesel engine, as Alvin shouts over it, "Luce's got the transport ready, hurry and we can get the hell out of here!"

He drags Ulrich toward the gap and up the ramp of the

M113. And I can taste the familiar air that circulates through the city of Enoch and hear the bustling of its population. It is all doused by the harmonious melody of singing that flows through the confines of the ship. I reach for Mandy but realize that she's strayed too far from my grasp. I turn around just in time to witness her sleek naked body stalk back into the veil of black.

I run after her, hoping to catch her hand and bring her to her senses. But I'm halted by a mass of forms, emerging from the gloom, taking up a combined radiance that turns their pallid skin to a ghostly luminance. Aramos stands in the middle with Seima standing flawlessly at his side. Mandy is drawn into the folds of the other Watchers – their name whispered to me in telepathic succession. They kiss her and caress her skin in an orgy of hands and arms. Aramos opens his arms to me, his earlier words echoing in my mind:

"We bring you the chance to sail the Solar Barque, we can give you secrets from the land of Nod."

Alvin rushes up next to me, having laid Ulrich just near the mouth, the pin cocked back on his rifle, "Quickly Harmon! She's one of them now, its time you and I gave these monsters what they deserve!"

I cannot explain what I see next, but caught between the realm of dreams and surreal I perceive the veil of this world lift. I see the raising of the celestial sails, the unfolding of angelic wings that spread beyond the boundaries of the ship, twinkling like the capture of a million stars! For a brief moment, I can see the end, the sorrowful fate of all humanity scintillating in those heavenly orbs as an unnatural calm drifts over my soul. In that instance, I feel the passing of years in utter isolation, floating through the mercy of heaven, lost to all those who I once held dear.

And in a unified choir I hear each of their voices call out, "Come, let us rejoice in the company of man."

Tears fall from my eyes as I raise the 38. I take my aim as if no control or will of my own. I hold my breath and fire the remaining rounds into Alvin's beautiful head.

I watch as they drive off, a harrowing look of betrayal and desolation from Luce's face as she, along with the desiccated husk of Ulrich Fontaine, disappear beneath the transports back hatch. Their fear, their horror, their madness now reflects like a dim star glittering in their eyes; reflecting but only a glimmer of the end of all things. The Watcher's hands and lips explore my body with lusting caress, pulling me like the ebb, back into the womb that is the Narthex. My mind adrift in a sea of limbs, hearing sounds and voices calling to me from the dark, I cannot help but wonder at what point, after traversing the heavens and meeting the cold of oblivion do we stop being human. Then again, I question, when did we ever start?

POEMS

Cycle of Mourners

Down into the depths of the sacred groves
Where the stones stand in shades
Into the lands where the ghosts all dwell
Marked where their corpses lay
The moaning tides of swollen mist
Release from hollowed trees
As nightly wrappings creep in whispers
Along the graves to be.
Plotted grounds of deepened soil
Sunk by greyish men
By earthly tool of darkest shovel
To bury a life again.
A tear to lose for mourners' sake
To honor the newly dead
Irony plays a horrid role
As each will share this bed.

Dance the Macabre

Pick up your mask my dear and
                Dance the Macabre
I have ridden for so long to reach
The ballroom floors,
So take my hand and
                Dance the Macabre
My journey was long and I
           Am tired,
But my feet are still strong.

Do not be shy, for my arms
              Are inevitable.
Embrace me and we shall
              Dance the Macabre
The night grows dim and the
Songs have waned.
So lay with me, darling…
              One last time.
For we have danced the macabre
And now our world grows black.

Envy

To loves, seek love, of endless grass
That shines on distant seas
A blight, sweet blight, and hollowed task
Leaving me in silent pleas.

Corrosive thoughts in endless wells
Dry in common tears
To whom they speak in blackened veils
And wallow in the mirrors.

Gothic Love Poem

And our spirits adorn in cappings
as our bones will do the waking;
And join in a harmonious gloom.

An when that day we renew our makings
and the ground will do its shaking
as, hand in hand, expel our tomb.

Life's Nurturing Embrace

Dripping pecks that bleed,
On crystal streaming roads,
Apart of visions seen,
And prophecies foretold.
Lives are but a thimble,
Whose finger allowed to cut.
In truth all have suffered,
Realities gruesome mock.
Yet waning moons trickle,
Across spinning wheels of time.
Our wounds do not heal,
The spokes caught in vines.
These leaves of halted misery,
Stem to bathe in light,
As darkness engulfs the roots,
Our past is lost in blight.
So awarded husks of torment,
The leaves darken and wither.
But never they crumble,
Aloft they smile and glitter.
Thus the wheel turns,
Amongst an orbiting hell,
Designed much in partial,
To become our worldly cells.
And as it rounds and rounds,
And spins our woes.
The stems of guilt,
Entangles the soul!
Faster and faster,
The leaves take hold,
Injecting monstrous pains,
And self-inflicting scolds.
And with one last turn,
The rotation stops,
Our own hand to the wood,
The wheel falls to rot.

Ode To Be My Darkling Child

Ode to be my darkling child,
My lady of blighted sun;
Cherished be in darken crypts
Longing for the touch of old.

I such a sweet bird and you a pearl in white,
carried in by the east; oh rising sun of mine.

The Demons danced in sepulchers,
Lain within my mind;
I myself, lost in wrappings
Crying for tears of beauty.

To rest in natures nest strewn high above the sea
Glistens as ever told, by bard, the sweetest lovely

Desperate be my dusted bones,
Lain a'strewn by past winters;
This lonely winter…
                    without you.

Oh Savage Night

Oh savage night that bleeds the marrow
Whilst thee are grey
Oh soothing song that sings my sorrow
That blocks my love of day.

Oh tempering winds that bathe my chances,
refute the lives its after
Oh troublesome hounds that prod with lances,
Prepare for sadistic laughter.

To scratch at tears and fallen branches
That hide in swollen pews.
Rest assured that love enhances
In radiant vibrant hues.

To call on storms and fleeting hearts,
To gather my soul in patches.
Born again to soar as larks,
As the forest blazes by matches.

Remember the Night When the Birds Above

Remember the night when the birds above
Sang of the skies and loving doves
The flew through the clouds in heavenly stride
But fell to the Earth for it was the stars that denied.

Chained to the ground, entangled in vines
Their wings were hindered, unable to fly.
As their feathers touched for one last goodbye
They were dragged far away, apart they would die.

Each moon that rose against the sky
Brought forth a tear in both doves' eyes.
Their hearts were empty as they looked far above
For how could life be without each other's love.

So they sang this song on that crippled night
When the moon was full, bathed in its light.
They sobbed their loss, their life now hollow
The days were clouded, engaged eternally in sorrow.

The Gear, Clock and Core

Woe sweet woe to pity my own inner core,
The songs of discord flow deep to travel the shore.
The inner workings of the crafty clock, ticking, ticking
To show the chipped gear grinding upon, grinding within.

I feel it working, climbing, grinding its way to climax
The mental stress picking at the brain
Peeling back layers of pain never to be felt before.
The pain, the pain the unbearable monstrosity of its lore,
To cause such torture of years upon years of scorn.

How came it by the inconceivable tools in store,
Those manly gifts of horror that destroy the core!
The toll, the toll, the striking of one,
The hardening of soul, faith and blood.

By Gods why have you forsaken this pitiful form?
Torn limb from limb couldn't hurt any more.
I feel the workings of the chimes collapsing within
Gears popping, strings dropping, the hands… stopping.

Yet, the clock soon starts ticking the famous song once more
Not smarter, not better, not special, to whom witness the gore!
But the gear still chipped passes the lever into its lonely dorm
Only to strike the hour within time, for which the clock is underscored.

The House with the Painted Door

Windows cracked
Glass now shattered
No dreams left to explore
Curtains tattered
Draperies rotted
In the House with the painted door.

Rusted nails
Floors all mangled
A life to live no more.
Webs entangled
Spiders all knotted
In the House with the painted door.

Creaking boards
Stairs in shambles
Tells of forgotten lore
Railing handles
Wood now blotted
In the House with the painted door.

Hallway paintings
Lifelike glares
Canvas lay all torn.
Maddening stare
Trails of blood.
In the house of gruesome gore.

Master's quarters
Locked with clasp.
An 'X' the wood now bore
Terrorized rasp
Head now snapped
In the house with the painted door.

The Love Once Lost

The bells toll a September night,
When memories were built in love.
A time of harmony, peace and friends,
When freedom flew as a dove.

Across a span of endless bliss,
Far beyond our worldly sight,
Grew tethered wings of fearsome feathers
That flew to a distant light.

Eternally bound for endless seas,
Drifting in a desolate pass,
The sun shone pure with rays of warmth,
This bird glistened as glass.

Tranquility marched to a heavenly beat,
As harmony was weaved in tune.
This dove hummed a beautiful song,
Surrounded by the clouds of gloom.

Jealousy sparkled in the eyes of winds,
They blew with astounding might.
This token of divinity, plucked from serenity
Fell deep, tumbling from flight.

Crying for forgiveness, her body not lifted,
The feathers twirled and clattered.
The rocks below grinned in pleasures,
Her penance only to shatter,

The bird's journey, a fading past,
The purity bled now ceases.
Alone to fathom these haunting memories,
The bells have crumbled to pieces.

The Spider of Six

Lo, sweet lo to the spider of six!
The crawling woe, of the midnight kiss.
Strike if one, be the others toil
Over the loss of their single spoil.

A bedrock stone, of harbored state
Kept in the glen where the widows mate.
Bound to the strands as a sacred device.
Immune to the powers of the spiders entice.

High, keep high the powers of six
The vicious crawler of thousands to list
One, but one, to carry the stone.
This macabre spider is only, and alone.

To Jealousy, I Engaged

Evil, dark, nightly forces
Flowing through the breeze
Stirring, stirring of countless souls
Trickling through the trees

Calling, moaning, shouting at the wind
Crying softly, endless tears
Pulling at my head, boiling, stirring,
Clawing at the mirrors.

Bites, nicks, grazing wounds
Seeping fresh at bosom's core
Stretching skin tightly, ghastly
Stricken to the floor.

Turning, turning screaming rage
Followed in spirits of regret
Flames flickering wildly, fury
Burning to forget.

Laugh to laugh, maddening gaze
Trampling blood to pain
Round and round, dashing, twirling
Stumbling onto shame.

(Continued on Next Page)

A pitch, a feather floating beyond
Painted to bear the gloom
Alone to suffer, tortured to see
Heading into inevitable doom.

Floating, hovering, minions of death
Eternal repetition to brave
Rambling, mumbling, screaming waste
Their love only I crave.

Echoes, echoes memories of the past
Besiege this husk enraged
Empty, shallow, pools of fate
To Jealousy, I Engaged.

Twisted Rhyming, Or You Are…

You are my firebrand, my destiny's sword;
Caressed in blackened flames, my gothic noir;
Assailed in petite embers, that dance n'pirouette;
A flash of immortality, cast n'shade an'silhouette;

You are my harbinger, my ultimate hero's boon;
Singing the call of eternity, a most harmonic tune;
You are my lightning cast, coursed n'mindful arc;
A jolted jig of tenebrous, illumed in purple spark;

You are my frozen tundra, my hollow winters night;
A mark of desolation, silence – a longing height;
I am your corrosive, a torture seeking acid;
An' you are the serene, the after closing placid;

You are my raining clouds, made in soot and tears;
Descending your roughly might, is music to my ears;
Beware the thunderclap, for which you run in hide;
The better part of beauty, is all when lacking pride;

You are my melodic winds, a beast or coveted sigh;
Impending lustful sailors, trapped n'ocean-by;
A hurricane or meek'fill gale, one in which to choose;
Horrid devastation I confess, my favored muse;

You are my trepid lover, a willful striding cat;
I am your humbled master, a milk in which to lap;
Together we are spurn'ful, dregs of commonality;
An' yet we are magical, a pair of a single amenity.

Untitled 7

Only the bones of carted silk can ever reach
The tip of a sword, to transgress into the seeds
Of demons and smile at diseased luxury.
To pass beneath trees of hallowed faith
And mournful grasses of wooden jars.
To display themselves before paper cutouts
And mock venomous visions that reflect
At them in mirrors.

They are the ones most worthy. Bred to
Achieve serrated spoils, bled from the hands
Of barren cults that are too lame to
Dissuade its assailants. Only towels
Can soak up the stains yet the pain
Still remains, to grow an empire of
Ash within the eyes of her neighbors.

The fortifications of companionship
Sewn together by crusts of bread are
Starved by dolls of happiness. Lodged
In servitude by a vagrant horse. Their
Pale fingernails scratch a notch of
Deviant dreams into the foreheads
Of cattle to rouse a grateful wince.

Rounded nose's sniff the tainted dust
Of playful nights, only to cough up
Home remedies to depression.
Eager to laugh at the foreign objects
Of lost antiquity addressed to
A long dead relative.
The holiday carols are just
Never the same.

Untitled

There is no God
The one who the bible sings
There are no angels
The ones with feathery wings
There is no Heaven
The one with silver bells
There is only punishment
The one we know as Hell.